Dear Mystery Reader:

After an exhaustive se[...] Press/PWA contest committee for the 7th Annual Best First Private Eye Novel, one writer clearly stood out against hundreds of competitors: Charles Knief. And when you read this mystery, I think you'll agree the committee was right on the money.

In DIAMOND HEAD, Charles introduces a fresh and compelling new PI to the mystery scene: retired U.S. Naval Officer John Caine. Living aboard his sailboat off the Hawaii coast, Caine does occasional "favors" for friends, usually simple ones like finding lost property or running risky errands. But when the daughter of one of Caine's close naval buddies is found raped and strangled to death, he finds himself obliged to figure out what happened. On a case that drags him through the seedy world of the snuff film industry, raging island fires, and even a run-in with some monster tiger sharks, Caine finds his normally tranquil world of sun and sand suddenly overshadowed by the grisly specter of murder.

With a debut performance reminiscent of John D. MacDonald and Robert B. Parker, DIAMOND HEAD is the first of what will surely be a successful, long-running series.

Yours in crime,

Joe Veltre
St. Martin's DEAD LETTER Paperback Mysteries

DIAMOND HEAD

CHARLES KNIEF

St. Martin's Paperbacks

This one is for Ildiko, who rescued me.

DIAMOND HEAD

Copyright © 1996 by Ildi Co.

Cover illustration by Roy Pendleton.

ISBN: 0-312-96547-8

Printed in the United States of America

St. Martin's Press hardcover edition published 1996
St. Martin's Paperbacks edition/March 1998

10 9 8 7 6 5 4 3 2 1

ΥΥΥΥΥΥΥΥ

ACKNOWLEDGMENTS

I am grateful to many people who helped in the creation of this novel. Rear Admiral Bill Cockle (Ret.), who knows every nuance of the United States Navy and assisted in technical matters; Maxíme Dougé, for his steadfast enthusiasm and for being a good friend in times both good and bad, here and there; Detectives Joyce Alapa and Mike Johnson, for letting me see inside the Honolulu PD (and for being there to watch my back when it really counted); Adrian Turley, for being a best friend who can always find the flaw; Bob Randisi and the Private Eye Writers of America, for being the first to see something special in the story; Ruth Cavin and the rest of St. Martin's editorial staff for their professional, patient and insightful guidance. There is something very special about these people. I am the better person for counting them as friends. It is a better book because of their association.

And I have to thank my children, Sarah, Abigail and Charles, for putting up with a missing father from time to time. I love you all.

Finally, this book would not have been completed without the unflagging support and love of my wife, Ildiko. No man could be more blessed.

from **"Shark Hula for Kalaniopu'u"**
(for Ka'lani'opu'u, uncle of King Kamehameha I)

Ka lālākea, ka manō ke'ehi 'ale,
Ka niuhi moe lawa 'o Ka-lani-'ōpu'u,
'O ka hō'elo'elo wela 'ole ia o ka maka,
'O ka umu ia nāna e hahao i ka 'ena'ena.
'O Ka-welo loloa nāna e ho'āliāli,
A 'a'ā'o Ka-lani-kau-lele ka hiwa.

O lalapa nō ka lāua keiki
'O Ka-pū-likoliko-i-ka-lani,
A kau maka manō, o ka maka 'anapa,
'O ka nanana i 'ō a i 'ane'i.

You are a white-finned shark riding the crest of the
     wave,
        O Ka-lani-'ōpu'u:
     a tiger shark resting without fear
     a rain quenching the sun's eye-searing glare
     a grim oven glowing underground:
        towering Ka-welo lighted it
           who caused Ka-lani-kau-lele, the Chosen,
           to blaze.

Their child was flaming Ka-pū-likoliko-i-ka-lani
she with the shark's face and flashing eyes
she of the restless questing gaze.

Reprinted by permission from *The Echo of Our Song:
Chants & Poems of the Hawaiians.* Translated & Edited by
Mary K. Pukui & Alfons L. Korn. University of Hawaii
Press, Honolulu, 1991.

1

The last two hundred yards of my daily run are always the hardest and that early summer evening was no different. It wasn't merely because the grade was all uphill; my mind was just about that far ahead of my body, anticipating the recovery, looking forward to a quick shower and a chilled glass of California chardonnay.

My feet pounded the asphalt past the Marina Restaurant. I stopped and walked the quarter mile to the joggers' fountain to warm down. There used to be a sign that marked it, but one of the patrons left the Marina early one morning and ran over it. Now the sign is gone and there's only a bubbler atop a galvanized pipe protruding from the lawn at a forty-five-degree angle.

I had been rounding back into shape after a six-month battle with injuries and indolence, the kind of injuries you get when you push your nose into other people's business and the kind of indolence when you're not certain you can start all over again. The first law of thermodynamics is even more certain as you approach your middle years. A body at rest does, indeed, tend to remain at rest.

The warmdown lasted until my heartbeat slowed to the legal limit and I could go home. Home is *Duchess*, a fifty-six-foot ketch-rigged sailboat I'd purchased in Singapore from a bankrupt Chinese merchant and sailed to Hawaii in the mid-eighties. *Duchess* is a generous lady, one of the few I have known. And for a while she'd been the only one in my life. I had been heading for California but got blown off course by a hurricane. By the time she was repaired I'd found my own patch of paradise and decided to stay.

Mine is the largest boat in the marina and draws the most water. Consequently she is farthest from the quay. I walked down the dock to my slip, watching the sky. The sunset was flaming, fluorescing the volcanic ash Kilauea was shooting from the south coast of the Big Island all the way into the stratosphere. Across Pearl Harbor's northern shore the water reflected gold and fiery red. Against the far mountains the last gasp of the day's cane harvest fires showed white against the black slopes, and black against the sky.

While watching the sunset I nearly missed seeing the bulky silhouette of a man sitting on *Duchess*'s stern, outlined against the evening sky. Even with his features in shadow I could tell he was big and fit, a carnivore, accustomed to occupying the top of the food chain.

"Good evening," I said in measured tones, angry at the trespass but not giving anything away. The way I earn my living sometimes causes me to make enemies. I live close and I live careful, and I've found it worthwhile to make some fast judgments before acting. The old body's not as quick as it used to be and my mind has learned to compensate for the slowing reflexes. "Anything I can help you with?"

"It's true what I heard about you white boys. You sure do sweat," said the man, his mature, gritty voice still heavy with the origins of his birth. It was a voice I immediately recognized. He stood and looked down at me, a benevolent, flashing smile adding another crease to the dark and fearsome face I knew so well. "Wipe yourself down, boy. I came by to have a drink with an old friend."

2

"Max!"

"It's been a long time, sailor."

"When did you get in?" I climbed into the cockpit and embraced the man who had been closer than any brother.

"This morning. You're a hard man to find, even on an island this size. Had to look for your boat. There's a master chief at the CPO club who covers for you pretty good. Had to show him my pedigree before he even admitted knowing you."

"Old friends."

"The only kind," he allowed. "You're getting back into shape," he said, punching me in the stomach with a playful jab.

"Starting to. Ran eight miles tonight."

"You might make it out of the wheelchair before long."

Max was dressed like a tourist in a tank top and shorts and white Nike lowtops with no socks. His T-shirt had startling green capital lettering that said HAWAII—IF IT SWELLS, RIDE IT!, pulled tight over hard muscle. He resembled a tourist the way a tiger shark resembles a goldfish. For a man in his late forties he was as solid as a rock. Hurricanes couldn't put him down.

Max pointed toward the restaurant above the boat slips. "They serve drinks up there at that shack?"

"Let me shower, then we'll talk."

I unlocked the cabin and went below to change. Max remained in the cockpit, catching the last rays of the warm summer sun on his face. He was still there when I returned, watching a small fleet of canoes racing to the buoy near the north shore of Ford Island. He wore a bemused expression of contentment.

Remembering how he had loved the local beer when we were stationed in Germany, I handed him a cold bottle of Edelweiss *Dunkel*. "Talk here. It's as good as any place and there's no cover charge."

Max accepted the beer, his smile widening. His eyes shifted from the sweating paddlers to me and back.

"This is peaceful, John," he said, his voice a reverent whisper, the way you'd speak in a cathedral. "You have truly found paradise."

"Had to get as far away from everywhere as I could."

"Did you find peace?"

"Close as it gets, I guess."

I piled some cushions against the opposite bulkhead and slid down against them. I was drinking my wine. I'd been thinking about the bittersweet flavor on my tongue during my run, been planning on drinking alone. But this was better.

"I have lately been to Europe," he said. "An all-expense-paid tour of the Balkans. You know the place. Where the First Big Mistake started when somebody shot some duke."

"Was it as bad as they say?"

"Worse, John. Worse than Lebanon. Worse than Somalia. We had no mission. The assholes put us out there for show one more time. A lot of good men died when the shooting started and they wouldn't back us up."

I hadn't been to Somalia, having left that life long before. But I'd been out *there* before, without backup from those whom Max had called "assholes." We'd been out *there* together more times than I could count. "Nothing more dangerous than your own politicians," I observed.

Max drank from the bottle, nodding and rolling his eyes in assent. "Goddamned whores are changing everything these days," he said. "But they never change. Probably been that way since the legions were marching along, rolling over all the known world in the name of Rome. But if they get in trouble . . ." His voice trailed off. "Soldiers don't change much. Neither do the politicians. Whores sell out the soldiers every time."

I let him drink and talk, unwinding from his travels. I knew he hadn't flown halfway across the Pacific just to look up an old shipmate and tell war stories. Max wasn't like that. He always had a mission.

"You still doing favors for friends?" he asked.

"When I need the money." Max never did accept the fact

that I'd pulled a private detective license in this state. He didn't think a living could be made that way. He called it "doing favors for friends." I didn't argue with him. In a way, that was how it seemed to work.

"How you fixed lately?"

"That depends."

Max took a last gulp from the Edelweiss, draining the bottle. "Depends upon what, the friend? How about me?"

"Just ask."

"You remember MacGruder?"

I remembered. He'd been our commanding officer once upon a time when it had been decided by our nation to waste thousands of its best and its brightest in an Asian war. He was the best of the best and the brightest of the brightest. He never let any of his men down. And when our country's politicians led us into yet another ill-considered and poorly conceived battle for a godforsaken piece of real estate in the South Caribbean he was there again, not for the glory or because he agreed with the cause, but because duty called. He'd always backed me up, and he had saved my life more than once. That last time he'd put his career on the line for me and my men. Our SEAL team had been pinned down by Cuban "construction workers" who just happened to have heavy automatic weapons and knew how to use them. He reversed the decision of a higher officer to abandon us and sent in a company of marines to relieve the pressure, allowing us to withdraw intact.

"Captain MacGruder?"

"Admiral now. Vice admiral. He's jumped a couple of pay grades since Grenada. That was the last time you saw him?"

I thought about it. "I guess it was." I left the navy soon after, unable to stomach the disaster the politicians were calling a victory. Too many of my best friends had died for the worst of reasons.

"Did you know he had a daughter? Lived here on Oahu?"

I shook my head.

"Named Mary. From what I knew of her she was a wild and beautiful girl. Chip off the old block but looked just like her mother. Graduated from Radford High. Then she went to some Ivy League college on the East Coast. After college she came back to Hawaii, because she loved it here when he had been assigned to CINPAC. Worked as a cocktail waitress in one of the big hotels in Waikiki. Got into some other stuff that wasn't so good."

"She okay now?"

"Depends upon your theology, I guess. Got herself murdered about three months ago. Raped and murdered. Left like some trash out on the Waianae coast."

"I hadn't heard about it."

"No reason for you to pay attention. You didn't even know she existed. I heard you were in pretty bad shape yourself about then, anyway." Max smirked at me. "Got it in the right leg again?"

"That was the one."

"What is that, three times in the same leg?"

"Twice, but that's enough."

He smiled and nodded. Through all the bad times Max had never been so much as scratched, as though bullets bounced off him. I'd caught most of it. More than once he'd taken my nearly lifeless body out of some hairy places, with hot, fast metal moving through our space, carrying me over his shoulder as if he were out for a jog in the park on a sunny day. Max, my Kevlar friend.

"Healing up pretty good now?"

"It's coming along."

"Could be you're getting kind of old to go whacking at windmills," he said. "Got another one of these?" He held up the dead soldier. I took the empty bottle below, pulled another beer from the cold locker and returned to the cockpit. The sky was a deep purple over the Waianae Mountains with night settling in. It was beautiful, but now I could only picture a dead thing beyond the distant peaks.

"Could be you're right, Max. I've got no other skills. Guess I could sell insurance."

"Guess you could, John, but it'd kill you. We're twins, you and me. I just stayed in, even though I'm old and tired. You got out because you couldn't stand the bullshit."

"So?"

"The police do not claim to have a suspect."

"What do you think I can do about it?"

"The admiral is a broken man. His wife died of cancer six months before his daughter was killed. You remember how he loved that woman? That hit him hard. I was there and it was a messy death. I thought that was going to do him in, but he's a tough old bird and he came through it pretty much intact. Then his only child was murdered. Now there's some nasty talk. About the daughter."

"Bad news?"

"The worst. The admiral wishes to pursue a political career when he retires. Something nasty surfaces about his kin, well, you know how campaigns are these days. Something like this would kill it."

"Politics? I thought you hated politicians."

"Every one of 'em since Ike."

"What do you want me to do, Max?"

"Someone's got to find the killer before the cops do. You're here. It's your island. It's what you do. No one else can be trusted." Max leaned forward, his voice softening. "You do favors for friends. I'm a friend. The admiral's a friend. We've all got history; we've seen it happen a time or two. The cops have their own agenda. Admiral MacGruder will need a friend looking out for his interests."

When I didn't react, he shook his head sadly and leaned back against the cushions.

"You might even come up with something the cops can't. You know people in the strangest places."

I nodded confirmation.

"And if you run across anything unfavorable about the girl, anything at all, lose it. Make sure it stays lost. Something nasty surfaces about the admiral's daughter, it'd finish him. Him and his military and political career."

"Why not have the Naval Investigative Service look into it. They're professionals. They can get all the information about the girl from the police."

"Aside from the jurisdiction problem, think about what you just said," said Max, settling against the cushions.

"The navy is a small institution, and anything they find out about the girl would soon be common knowledge."

He nodded. "Nobody keeps a secret anymore, John. Only friends do. Those boys and girls would hand the results of their investigation upstairs and one of the admiral's enemies would get hold of it and it would be certain to leak. There's only one way to keep secrets. Limit the knowledge. To friends."

Max was handing me two missions. First, find the killer, and then make sure anything about the girl that could damage her father would never see the light of day. There could be only one way to ensure that.

"I'm not an assassin."

"Not without good cause, anyway."

I winced, remembering a time in Central America when I was ordered to do so, and Max had worked support.

"I wouldn't know where to start . . ."

"You owe him, John."

"We both do," I said.

"That's why I took a couple of days leave. It took me all day to find you. I have to be back in Coronado tomorrow night. I can't do anything about this. Not while I'm in uniform. But you can."

"All right, what can it hurt?" Max was right. I had a debt to pay.

ⅤⅤⅤⅤⅤⅤⅤⅤ

2

We went to the Marina Restaurant for plates of ribs and greasy fried chicken, steak fries and coleslaw, a real Hawaiian feast. We washed it down with cold bottles of Tsing Tao, toasts to absent companions and old sea stories. Max brought me current with the old bunch of guys who, it turned out, were actually a bunch of new guys I'd never heard of. Most of the men we'd served with had either retired, been promoted or died. Max was the only one left.

Max had lately been running groups through SERE Camp, a quaint little naval installation in the hills of northern San Diego County. SERE stands for survival, evasion, resistance and escape. Navy pilots are sent there to learn how to counter the physical and psychological torture they can expect if they get shot down in the Third World, the only place where military people ply their trade these days. Max reminded me that the first time we'd ever seen SERE Camp, we'd been together.

The marines ran it then. They'd taken five SEALs from Coronado, blindfolded us and dropped us off one by one in the middle of the night in the hills surrounding the camp, instructing us to stay low until the next morning. Before they abandoned us to the bush they kicked us, mocked us and swore at us in Cuban-Spanish and Russian. I remembered them as a jolly bunch. As they beat us they laughed a lot. The idea was that no matter how hard we'd try to hide they'd capture us.

That was the idea. They were elite recon marines, used to dealing with pilots who were accustomed to sitting in their weapons, not carrying them. We gave them something to think about. By 2300 we'd rounded up all twenty-eight of our "captors" and controlled the camp. That night was the cause of a policy change at SERE. Never again did they send more than two SEALs. If they send any at all now, they double the marines.

After dinner I drove Max to Hickam Air Force Base where he squeezed onto a MAC flight to Alameda in California. He'd hop a civilian carrier from there to San Diego and be home by tomorrow morning. He wanted to clear the island. He didn't want to be around when I started stirring up a cloud of dirt. From what he'd told me, that was a possibility. He had nearly thirty years in and wanted to retire with a clean slate. I didn't blame him, but I wished he could have stayed. If there was anyone out there with murderous intent, there's no one I'd rather have watching my back.

Max's C-141 lifted from the runway just before midnight. Watching the big cargo jet arc over the lagoon, a realization hit me like an adrenaline rush that a hole in my life had been filled. I'd been irritable lately, restless and bored. Tired of my own company. The physical training had been challenging, bringing me back to within a few notches of my top form, but training for training's sake is dulling after a while. Max had done me a favor by asking for one of his own.

I didn't know much about murder investigations, but it seemed that a good place to start would be to find out what the police knew. They'd have a file, rich with information. I only knew two ways to get a look at a police file. I could ask the police, but I didn't think they'd give me any cooperation, or Chawlie could get me a copy.

Leaving Hickam I got on the eastbound Nimitz Highway toward downtown Honolulu instead of heading back to Pearl Harbor. My old Rolex said it was twelve-twenty. It would take me five minutes to reach Chinatown and another fifteen to find a parking place, but there was no hurry. Unless he was dead, my man would be in his usual spot until well after three in the morning.

Hotel Street used to be the center of Honolulu's red-light district. During World War II there were no fewer than a hundred and fifty houses of prostitution within the ten square blocks of Chinatown. Now the area is mainly a tourist attraction with lei stands, Chinese, Filipino and Vietnamese restaurants, and not a red-light house in sight. They're still there. You just have to know where to look.

The man I wanted to see was around the corner on River Street, a wandering road named for the meandering stream called Nu'uanu that bordered Chinatown's western edge. I don't know his real name. He's known to me only as Chawlie. Chawlie can be found every night on a hard plastic chair in the foyer of the small restaurant facing the bronze statue of Dr. Sun Yat-sen, fifteen paces from the Nu'uanu Stream.

Most people seeing the old man in the threadbare clothes might think he is there to share the rice bowl of the restaurant, an uncle fallen on hard times perhaps, living off the largess of a successful family. In reality he owns the rice bowl, the restaurant and possibly half of Chinatown. Chawlie knows everything that happens in town, both above and below the legal lines. Most recent politicians from the City and County of Honolulu have come to him for substantial financial help in their campaigns. There is an understanding, of course, that Chawlie will get whatever he wants in the way of city assistance for rezoning or building permits or whatever else he wants whenever he wants it. Chawlie doesn't speak Latin but he understands *quid pro quo*.

I heard somewhere that Chawlie's net worth approaches two hundred million dollars.

Chawlie likes me. I don't see him much, maybe that's why. A couple of years ago he had a delicate problem he couldn't resolve without outside help. A "professional" woman got her hooks into him and tried to shake him down in return for what she had learned about the old man's bedroom habits. He's a proud man. Going to one of his many lawyer nephews might have solved the problem, but would have exposed a weakness. Seeking help from a *haole* lawyer was even worse. Reporting the extortion to the police was unthinkable. He needed to get the woman off his back in the quickest and most discreet way possible. Someone recommended my services to him. I'm an outsider, not of the clan. Somehow he found that reassuring.

For a small fee I handled his problem. The lady left the island, happier and somewhat richer than she had been before, but not as rich as she had planned. Nobody ever knew what it was Chawlie liked that got him in trouble. No one found the one piece of information that might have started his empire crumbling. I think at first he expected me to come back to him for more than just my fee, to exploit what I alone knew about him. It didn't happen. Now Chawlie introduces me as ". . . John Caine. He haole, but he okay." It's his highest accolade.

I found him perched primly on an orange plastic chair, gazing into the night.

"Good evening, Uncle," I said respectfully.

Almond eyes tracked my approach, no expression on the face they inhabited.

"I see you, John Caine," said Chawlie, finally acknowledging my presence. "How are you feeling?"

"My health is good, Uncle."

Chawlie looked me up and down, as if appraising the veracity of my claim. At last he pointed to another chair, a companion to his own.

"Sit," he commanded. When I obeyed, he smiled. "You no

come see me. Two years you go away from this place and not return. I know you here on island. All time I wait for you to come and ask me what about this, what about that. I know what you do and I know you need my help. I say to myself, This John Caine, he will want something someday. He come to me then." The eyes twinkled with merriment. "So. What you want, haole? You need money?"

"No, Uncle," I said, shaking my head. "I have no need of your money."

"Everybody need money. But that's good you not want any because I no loan money to you. You not live so long, I think. You let people shoot you. Somebody kill you next time, you no pay me back."

"I need a file. A police file."

"You think I can get police file? Are you stupid?"

"I know you can, Uncle. If you want to."

Chawlie studied me, his face impassive. I leaned back in my chair and waited.

"What kind police file?" he said after a while.

"Homicide, Uncle."

"Oh, homicide! Something simple! Homicide police file! You know I cannot get a police file. And a homicide file! You must think Chawlie can do anything!"

I nodded. "Yes, Chawlie. In this town I think you can."

The face remained impassive but I knew I'd pleased him. "It is big problem."

He watched my face for a reaction. I gave him nothing.

"It would cost much money. If I could get one for you."

"How much money, Uncle?"

"Five thousand dollars."

"When can you get it?"

"I never say I get it. Did I say I get it?"

"I can have five thousand dollars here by tomorrow noon."

"Tomorrow night. Here. Same time."

"Midnight."

He nodded. "What name is on the file?"

"The victim's name is MacGruder. First name Mary. A young female. She was killed and left near Waianae about three months ago. I don't know anything else about the case. I was hoping the file would enlighten me."

"Take more than police file to enlighten you."

I had been dismissed.

"Thank you, Uncle." I got up to leave.

"John Caine!"

I turned. The old man was sitting as still as a statue.

"Stay awake tonight. Mebbe somebody will come to your boat with a package."

"I'll be awake."

"And you be here tomorrow night with the money."

"I will, Uncle. Midnight. I'll bring the money."

"Cash!" said Chawlie, the trace of a smile dancing across his lips. "No checks!"

"Cash," I repeated.

"And don't let anyone kill you before you pay!"

VVVVVVVV

3

Dawn was still an hour away when a subtle shift in *Duchess*'s motion woke me from a dreamless slumber. My visitor was awkward and clumsy, and from the sound of the hard soles scuffing my teak deck, a stranger to a marine environment. I opened the hatch and invited the intruder in.

My visitor carefully climbed down the ladder, putting both feet on each step before attempting the next one. That was about all she could do in a skintight silk dress and four-inch spike heels. As she descended, it was obvious her dress contained a spectacular body.

"You are Mr. Caine?" She had a face to match her body and a voice to melt butter. This was a real dragon-lady–bitch-goddess.

"I am."

"This for you." The tiny goddess handed me twelve inches of photocopied pages. Chawlie had been as good as his word.

"Thank you. Chawlie sent you?"

She answered the question by alighting on the lounge settee and adjusting her stockings. They were honest-to-God stockings, not panty hose—I could see smooth flesh. She was exquisite in dress and feature, a rich man's toy, and the business with the stockings had been an intentional act. Not an invitation, just a demonstration: *I am unattainable for one such as you. But I can show you what you are missing.* Slouched against the bulkhead in cutoff sweatshirt and shorts, I felt like a peasant. When she stood and reached her full height I noted that the top of her head barely reached the middle of my chest. God knows what she'd been told about me, but she'd been expecting rape or worse.

"Uncle say to be careful until tomorrow night. He will be waiting for you. I go now." English was not her native tongue. I wondered if Chawlie had smuggled her into the country for his private consumption or if she was a prime choice from a regular load. I decided she must have been handpicked for the old man from the beginning; she was too perfect.

I extended my hand to assist her as she addressed each step of the ladder and I followed her up on deck to make sure she made it safely to the dock without falling overboard. When her spike heels touched the relatively stable surface of the dock she took off like a rocket. I watched her until she disappeared beyond the darkened restaurant, the sound of her hard little heels tapping a staccato beat against the concrete. I heard a car door shut and saw the profile of a large, dark sedan leave the parking lot.

One of Chawlie's women. She would be heading back to his bed, escorted by a keeper or two. She would report, and would be rewarded for her courage in entering the haole's lair.

It's a tossup who's more racist, the Japanese or the Chinese. Either one makes the KKK seem as innocuous as Barney. My vote is for the Chinese. They view themselves as the only human race. The Mandarin word for the Chinese people is *han,* meaning "human beings." No one else qualifies. And yet they have been discriminated against throughout the rest of the world. Most people do not know that the Vietnamese boat people of the late seventies were nearly all ethnic Chinese, descendants of a great diaspora eight hundred years earlier. Though they had lived in Vietnam for eight centuries, they had not intermarried and had retained their ethnic and cultural identity. The Chinese have a strong sense of family and a great appreciation of education, and they became entrenched in the arts, in medicine, in the bureaucracies. And they were sorely hated by the Vietnamese. The feeling was mutual. Chinese do not like outsiders. Chawlie deals with me only because I have a commodity he can acquire nowhere else: absolute trust.

I could have given the woman the money to take to Chawlie, but I wanted no one to know I kept that kind of cash aboard. I don't trust anyone that much. I'd see him at midnight and make a show of going to the bank before. But nearly every thing I owned was on this boat, ready to leave in a moment's notice.

The stack of photocopied files lay on the lounge table demanding my immediate attention. I made a pot of Jamaican Blue Mountain as the sun rose over Makalapa Hill, and started working.

So how do you find a murderer? Police will tell you nearly every homicide is the result of a dispute between people who knew each other. Lately Hawaii has experienced more of the random violence that is engendered in the squalor of the big mainland cities—serial killings and drive-by shootings—strangers killing strangers. This didn't feel like that kind of killing. There hadn't been anything in the newspapers about a local serial killer and it may not have been random. The chances were good the killer's name was contained in the file, or that there was a lead to the man who did it.

I found the medical examiner's report. There was semen in the vagina, type AB positive, not the rarest of blood types, but not common either. It is less rare in Asians. There was evidence of bruising of the external genitalia, but that didn't mean anything either. Pubic hairs combed from the body were found to be ovoid in shape and therefore Asian. There were ligature marks on the wrists and ankles, tight enough to have broken the skin. Lacerations on the buttocks, elbows and upper back, with splinters of Wolmonized Douglas Fir embedded in the flesh, was evidence the victim had been tied to a cross-brace formed like a giant X. One page showed a detailed drawing of such a construction. The depth of the strangulation cord, up to a half inch deep into her flesh, told how she died. It was an ugly picture. A young, vital woman used up and thrown away, decades of bright future squandered. And for what?

There is never an answer to that question. Never a satisfying answer, anyway. Too often, it comes back simply: *Because*.

I put the medical examiner's report aside. I quickly sorted through the copies of photographs that went with it. They did not make me want to linger. A blood-darkened face with the jutting black tongue gave no hint of the beauty that must have been there. I shuddered, imagining what kind of horrors these pictures must have given MacGruder had he seen them. He had bounced this nightmarish thing on his lap when it was a golden-haired pixie with big blue eyes; had been there when the tot cut her first tooth; had looked on in awe when she spoke her first word. And now this. I hoped he had been shielded from these photographs. They were enough to make a man stop believing in a god but not enough to make a man stop believing in the devil.

I turned the photographs over. They could tell me nothing now.

I read through all of the detectives' narratives. There was a faint whiff of a suspicion of narcotics somewhere in the investigation, but nothing definite. I went back to the forensic file.

Examination of the knots was inconclusive. The knots used on her hands and arms were square knots, different from the ones on her ankles. Those were granny knots, indicating that the person who tied the cord at her feet was either untrained or had been a different person from the one who tied her hands, or both. The direction of the knots hinted that the one who tied her hands may have been left-handed. Toxicological tests came back negative for drugs. There was only a trace of alcohol. I didn't see where drugs could be involved. Perhaps it was because there wasn't any evidence directly relating to drugs. Perhaps it was because I've learned that where there's smoke, there could be a smoke screen.

I poured my last cup of coffee and went out on deck. The sun was shining proudly behind a low band of clouds scudding across the sky. Rain in the mountains above Pearl Harbor gave me a rainbow, arching over Pearl City and Makakilo. The clouds would go away and the sun would stay, and it would be another perfect, beautiful day.

What did you do, little girl, I thought, that got you into so much trouble? Who were you running with that did that to you? There were no answers. There was only the breeze, slapping the rigging against the mast.

Someone had profited from her death. That was an assumption, a logical place to start. No one but a thrill killer does this unless there is a profit. Could the profit have been pleasure? It was plausible. There are some sick people out there and she had been ill-used before her death. Could it have been a rough game gone bad? Perhaps. She was young and strong, and I could not imagine how a man could have forced her to get on the X-brace without her cooperation. Even two men. Could the profit have been something else? Something like guaranteed silence? Protecting what? Nothing in the file specifically stated anything about her behavior. But implications were everywhere.

I went below and forced myself to look at the photographs again. She had been discarded on the rocky coastline near the mouth of the Shark Cave, north of Makaha. That's rough country, rough in the sense that blond haoles like me just do not go there at night. It's also Hawaiian Homelands, rural slums set aside for descendants of the original inhabitants of these islands. Was someone trying to shift the blame to the people who lived out there?

Years back, a band of Samoans rampaged through the area,

killing haoles sleeping on the beach, but they had been an aberration and were quickly caught and convicted. This was not that kind of thing. Mary had been killed somewhere else and dropped there. And the location had been for a reason.

I dug out my map book of Oahu. The Shark Cave is a legendary lava tube halfway between Makaha and Kaena Point, the end of the road. There is no way even a sturdy four-wheel drive can make it around the point to the other side anymore. The roadway used to be the route of the old cane railway, but the tracks were removed more than fifty years ago and the roadbed eventually washed out. It's as close to nowhere as you can get on this island.

The file had not been illuminating. The interviews and narratives were too vague, filled with sparse and unintelligible references to files not available to me. There was something going on here, but I couldn't afford to ask for more files from Chawlie. I needed to speak to the lead investigator on the case. But first I needed to see the place where the body had been found.

I did my morning exercises and took a quick shower, washing away the cobwebs. Lately I'd dropped to my fighting weight of 190 pounds. I'm not a heavyweight. I don't have the bone structure. For most of my adult life I've drifted between 185 and 210 pounds. Once or twice, when I got real lazy, I ballooned up to 220. The effort to get back to my prime weight gets harder every year. The effort to maintain it is less difficult than allowing myself to lose control and get sloppy again. Staying in shape is actually taking the path of least resistance. When I finally give up and get totally out of shape I'll have to retire. There's no way I can stay in this business and not be in top physical condition. Not with the creatures out there I have to deal with.

So at my age I tend to stay close to my optimal weight, watch what I eat and restrict my alcohol to two glasses of wine a day. And I don't drink those unless I've earned them. To earn them I have to do my MDR—minimum daily requirement—of two hundred push-ups, two hundred sit-ups and an eight-mile run. I like to eat the rare steaks and I like the sauces the good chefs make, and if I don't do the exercise I start to get soft within two weeks.

That's my biggest fear. I hate being soft. All my life I've been the guy people instinctively run to for help. It wouldn't fit my self-image to have to run to someone else. So I do the reps every morning and I pay my dues at sundown every night. Psychologists would have a field day with me until they found out why I do it. Then they'd be out there with me, pushing me for that extra mile.

4

Other than *Duchess* and a ten-speed bike, my only transportation is an ancient, military-issue, World War II Jeep. Four-speed, four-wheel drive, it's a 1944 Willys. Not a Chrysler. Not even American Motors. This is the original gosh darned *Jeep*. The only concession to its civilian status is its battleship gray paint. It gets thirty-four miles to the gallon and has a top speed of fifty-six miles per hour, which is perfect for this island. If you go any faster, you're in danger of driving off land's end.

It was a long drive past Makaha on the Leeward Coast. Oahu is a small rock in the middle of a big ocean. Most of the state's population resides on this island, and most of them are in Honolulu. Away from the population center Oahu is just like the rest of the state: rural, agricultural, and with notable exceptions, relatively poor. The Leeward Coast is one of the poorest on the island. Little rain falls there. The rain-giving clouds drop most of their moisture on the eastern slopes of the Waianae Mountains. That's good for Dole and C&H Sugar, but it's bad for the residents of Waianae and Makaha. Most of the Leeward Coast resembles a slum in the desert. A desert possessed of the most beautiful and uncrowded beaches on this planet, but a desert all the same.

Few tourists make it to the Leeward Coast. There's only one

road to and from, and it takes over an hour from the hotel district by car. At Kaena Point, a rugged arrow of land jutting into the Pacific, you're as far from civilization as you can get. There are no amusement parks, no hotels, no cultural centers, no attractions of any kind to lure the tourists from Waikiki and the North Shore.

It's probably a good thing there aren't too many tourists. They're not particularly welcome on the Leeward Coast. The word *makaha* means "fierce" in Hawaiian, and the story goes that long before Captain Cook met King Kamehameha a tribe of cannibals lived in Makaha. They would wait for the occasional traveler making his way along the coast and then attack, kill and eat him. People have been killed for their cars there. The local police station is called "the Alamo," in reference both to its Spanish-fortress architecture and to an attack by the locals a couple of years ago. The place just does not have the Aloha spirit that tourists have come to expect.

I took it slow through the towns of Nanakuli, Waianae and Makaha. Nanakuli is just a cluster of small homes, but Waianae is a relatively large town. It has restaurants, banks and a mini-mall. It even has a McDonald's. Makaha is an outpost. There is a luxury hotel the residents of Honolulu use when they want to get away from it all, and there's a condominium complex way up in Makaha Valley whose location defies all logic. Aside from that, the town of Makaha is a collection of corrugated-metal-roofed shacks along the beach.

I didn't know what I thought I would find. The crime was more than three months old. Forensic experts had gone over the site for any evidence that might have been there. I didn't expect to find clues. I just wanted to see the layout for myself, and to imagine what it would have been like when the body was dumped.

I pulled the Jeep onto the dirt strip near the Shark Cave. There weren't any other cars parked in the immediate area. Across the road an old man was fishing, the line from his pole lying atop calm turquoise water. We were the only people in sight.

I climbed down from the Jeep and entered the cave. The entrance was forty to fifty feet across and more than twenty feet high, soaring overhead like a cathedral, then dropping to meet an insignificant hole in the ground reminiscent of where the rabbit went in *Alice in Wonderland*. I recalled what the place was like inside from a visit I had made out of curiosity one bright afternoon a few years back. The ground was littered with aluminum cans and the assorted detritus of modern civilization, including an occasional condom. Graffiti adorned the rock walls.

I took the photographs of the body from the file and tried to orient myself to the glossy black-and-white background. I got lucky and found the spot almost immediately. Mary Mac-Gruder's corpse had not been left inside the cave, but just at its mouth. From the way her legs and arms were splayed I could tell she'd been casually tossed to the ground like a discarded cigarette.

I imagined it as it had to have happened. The car pulled off the paved road, the driver getting as close as he could to the cave. He couldn't get to the entrance because it was blocked by big lava boulders. Those same boulders also obstructed the view from the road. Mary's corpse had been hoisted up and over the rocks and left on the sheltered side. The car turned around and went back toward Makaha. The road to the north dead-ended near Kaena Point, so there was nowhere else they could have gone.

The whole operation would have taken less then fifteen seconds to accomplish. There were at least two men, one to drive and one to wrestle the body from the vehicle and over the boulder. Taking a dead woman from a car would not be easy. Even an open vehicle such as a pickup or a Jeep would have presented problems. So what did they use?

There was only one answer that came to mind: the serial

killer's best friend, the van. With cargo doors on the passenger side and at the rear, vans have been the choice of terrorists, serial and professional killers for over three decades.

It wasn't much. It was merely an insupportable supposition. Yet my instinct told me I was right. It wasn't anything, but it was a start.

I left the cave, the file under my arm.

And froze in place.

Two young men were sitting in my Jeep. One had broken open the glove compartment and was rummaging through its contents. The other was busy with both hands buried beneath the dashboard. They were big, they were young, and they were trying to steal my Jeep.

I set the file down behind a rock, stepped out of my sandals and approached from the driver side.

I wasn't worried about the Jeep. No matter what they tried they couldn't start it. I'd installed a disabler on the starter. There's no alarm, because I think they're useless and needlessly irritate, but a little infrared transmitter on my key chain disables the engine when I push the button. A would-be thief couldn't start it even if he had a key. I only kept insurance and inspection records in the glove box, but I didn't appreciate the attempt.

"Any luck?" I asked.

The youth looked at me, startled. He hadn't heard my approach. "Who're you?" he asked. The other thief sneered, trying his best to intimidate.

"Haole fuck," he answered for me.

"That's my Jeep," I said. "Who're you?"

"Fuck 'dis." The driver shoved hard against my chest. I backed away from his hand and his momentum carried him. He tumbled onto hard-packed ground, landing on hands and knees.

"Careful," I said. "You're going to hurt yourself."

The other young man came around the back of the Jeep,

25

carrying something in his hand. I watched him approach, my hands on my hips, mindful of the driver struggling to his feet.

"Don't get in over your head," I warned the one coming at me. He held a short tire iron. His intentions looked far from peaceful.

I'd already decided on *aikido*, a form of martial arts that has no attack, and I centered myself for what was to come. These two were young and probably had no experience in fighting, but I saw an innate meanness of spirit, too. They looked like they got through life by bullying whatever came their way. They looked as if another lesson in mean would not teach them anything they hadn't already absorbed. One more ass-kicking more or less probably would not matter in the overall scheme of their lives.

The one with the tire iron swung it overhead and brought it down where my skull had been. By the time it came full arc I was behind and beside him, catching his wrist in both hands, continuing the swing of his arm until he rolled onto his back. I released his hand before the shoulder broke, but twisted the weapon until it came free.

I tossed it over the road into the sea.

The one who had been in the driver's seat was now on his feet, scrambling toward me.

The passenger got up and clubbed at me, his fist traversing thin air. I assisted his turn, pirouetting him into his partner. They slammed together and sat down hard. It would have been comical had they not been so intent on caving in my head and stealing my vehicle.

"This is ridiculous," I said as they got up. "Nobody's been hurt yet. Let it rest."

"Haole fuck," said the one who had used the pry bar, seemingly stuck on that one expression. He leaned against the side of the Jeep, feeling around the footwell, apparently looking for a weapon of some kind. The driver hung back, unsure, as if the fight was gone from him.

"Go on home," I told them. "Have a beer. No harm done."

"Fuck you, haole." Having found nothing, the passenger launched himself at me, both meaty hands grabbing for my throat.

I moved to the side and let him run past. He stumble-stepped a couple of strides, tripped over his own feet, and sprawled onto his stomach.

I turned toward the driver, but he backed away, his hands in front of his body to ward me off.

"Go!" I shouted, taking a step toward him.

He fled.

Something hit me on the shoulder with nearly enough force to knock me down. I ducked as another baseball-size stone zinged by my head. A third kicked up a cloud of dust near my feet. The thief with the limited vocabulary and a propensity for hitting people with hard objects was pitching lava rocks at me as fast as he could pick them up. He had an almost unlimited supply where he was positioned, near the mouth of the cave.

So much for good intentions.

I charged into the barrage, zigzagging as best I could, avoiding most, but not all of the stones. One hit me in the chest and another staggered me when it glanced off my knee. As I neared, he abandoned the rocks and retreated into the cave. I followed, catching him from behind.

Two blows to the side of his throat felled him. He collapsed, graceless as a sack of cement. I checked him for vital signs. He wouldn't die, I had pulled my punches. I left him on the floor of the cave. It was cooler there, out of the sun.

I retrieved the file and my sandals and went to the Jeep. It took about five minutes to repair the damage done to the ignition switch, and to realize I'd thrown my own tire iron into the Pacific. Before I left I checked the young man in the cave again. He would awake soon and be able to prey on his fellow humans some other day. He might even improve his language skills.

Of the other thief there was no sign.

I smugly congratulated myself on the outcome of the battle. I'd taken my lumps and had given a few; one foe was vanquished, the other fled. They'd been warned early on. Only their persistence had caused them hurt. That they were both at least a quarter century younger was satisfying for the moment.

But as I drove back toward Pearl Harbor I still felt as if I'd kicked the family dog.

5

I t was too soon to talk to the detective in charge of the case. I didn't yet know enough to ask intelligent questions. My level of understanding wasn't what it should have been, and only a dose of old-fashioned hard work would remedy that deficiency.

According to the file, Mary MacGruder had worked in one of the hotels along Waikiki Beach. The place was one of the landmarks of Hawaii, and once upon a time I'd spent a pleasant week playing tourist there with a woman I'd hoped might be the love of my life. She would have been, were I willing to settle down to a forty-hour week, pension plan, health benefits and a 401-K. She hadn't made those demands. She hadn't made any, but she'd expected me to make the offer, and the absence of the offer hung there between us until she got smart and went back to the mainland. I was another disappointment in her life, a familiar part for me to play.

The hotel had seven bars, and with the sun going down it wasn't the worst assignment I'd ever given myself, moving from bar to bar, nursing white wine and making small talk with the waitresses to find someone who might have known the admiral's daughter. The turnover in those places is high, but there's always one waitress who's been there since they poured the foundation, and in the third bar I tried, the one on the lanai next to the white sand beach, I found Louise.

My table was about the size of a cocktail tray, wedged against some boulders between two palm trees. The bar was crowded and Louise was busy hustling drinks, but she was the kind of waitress who could talk fast and serve fast and never lose her nerve or her memory. I vaguely remembered her as a cocktail waitress from my romantic interlude here. Hers was a personality that sticks with you. You get the service, you get what you order, and if you're any kind of interesting at all, you'll get fast, popping sarcasm to go with it. If anyone would remember Mary MacGruder, it would be Louise.

Security guards were shooing people off the beach while carpenters assembled a portable stage on the sand in front of the bar. Most of the big hotels have some kind of commemoration marking the end of another day in paradise. The Hilton Hawaiian Village shoots fireworks over its own lagoon and the Royal Hawaiian has a luau, complete with a roasted pig. I didn't know what this hotel had planned for the event, and I didn't care. The bar would be packed until the show was over, and then it would be deserted as the tourists sought their celebration elsewhere. I gave up my table to a young sunburned couple wearing matching Aloha shirts and new rings on the third fingers of their left hands.

I removed my sandals and walked along the edge of the Pacific, watching the sun go down beyond the reef. It was another of nature's spectaculars, something we expect as an entitlement as *Kama'aina*, children of the land. Clouds drifting south from Barber's Point reflected a limitless, flamingo orange-pink sky.

My shoulder ached. My knee hurt. Max had warned me I was getting too old for this. Maybe he was right. He would know better than most. It didn't bring me joy, banging on those car thieves, and it didn't bring satisfaction, either. Violence always left a bitter aftertaste, a bile from the soul. But I wouldn't deny that part of me, either.

After the incident at the Shark Cave I went to my bank to visit my safe deposit box. There isn't any money there, that's aboard *Duchess*, but if Chawlie had anyone watching me I didn't want him reaching the right conclusion. I carried a day pack with a few odds and ends and the five thousand dollars in cash. The fifty bills were a heavy load inside the pocket of the pack.

I am not normally a nervous person. Two or three times I've carried more cash in places where the locals would have happily cut my throat for fifty cents American. But that money belonged to someone else and it was back in the bad old days when I needed an adrenaline rush with every job. The "crank" was as necessary for me as the income. I no longer am an adrenaline junkie. Having that kind of cash money makes me jumpy. And things have changed here. Parts of the island are no longer safe at night. Roaming gangs of vicious children are beating, robbing and raping both tourists and residents, choosing their victims with equanimity. Elementary-school arsonists are setting the mountains on fire. Waikiki no longer has the harmless Disney atmosphere it had ten years ago. At night, Kapiolani Park feels like Central Park.

I'm not particularly worried about my own safety, but it was a comfort knowing the money would be out of my hands in a few hours.

The memories and the sunset and the newlyweds and the alcohol combined to make me maudlin, and I wondered about the woman I had disappointed. I remembered her walking away from me near this very spot, marching off with a stiff back, her head held high. That she was better off without me was a foregone conclusion. She thought I could have been right for her, but she didn't really know me and there were too many qualifiers. I knew she wasn't The One. I'd loved that one long ago, and they'd killed her.

I cut through Fort DeRussey and wandered back down Kalakaua Avenue toward the hotel when I judged the sky was dark enough and the crowds were thinning along the beach.

When I got to the entrance of the hotel I found I'd judged it right. Feeling like a salmon on a spawning run, I bucked against the pedestrian traffic flooding onto the street.

The bar was empty of patrons. The sun was gone and so was the view, replaced by a vast darkness. Louise was leaning against the bar, resting her elbows on the ceramic tile, easing her back and her feet. She watched me enter the bar with such visible mixed emotions it made me smile.

"I'll sit at the bar," I told her. "Make it easy on you." I slipped onto the bar stool next to the waitress station.

She smiled and didn't move, her weariness and gratitude both visible. "What'll you have, sugar?" She had a voice constructed of equal parts Louisiana bayou, cigarettes and cheap whiskey.

"Chardonnay."

"You were here earlier. You stayin' here?"

"No, ma'am."

She leaned toward the bartender, who'd heard the conversation. He nodded and reached for the house bottle.

"Six fifty," she said, placing the wine on the tile in front of me. I handed her a twenty and told her to keep the change.

"Kinda steep, ain't it?" she asked, instantly wary.

"Cost of doing business," I said.

"Expense account, huh? You working?"

"Looking for information on a girl who used to work here. Thought you might have known her."

"I probably do, mister," said Louise. "And if I do, it's probably best if you don't ask."

"This girl was killed about three months ago. She worked here before then, but I don't know when or how long."

"That MacGruder girl? The one that was in all the papers? That's the one you mean?"

I nodded.

"That poor little thing." She looked at me again, this time really appraising me and my clothing. I'd changed at the boat, putting on my best shorts and a long-sleeved white Egyptian cotton shirt with straps on the sleeves so you could roll them up and secure them with a button. It was the equivalent of my Sunday best. "You a cop?"

"I'm looking into the matter for the family," I said. It was the truth, as far as it went.

"Some kind of a private cop?"

"Just doing a favor for a friend."

"You ain't no tourist. I knew that right off. Thought you were military, the way you move, the shape you're in, that 'ma'am' stuff." She pursed her lips. "Look, sugar. You've got an honest face, but the management here don't like me chawin' with the customers, if you know what I mean? I get off in about thirty minutes, soon as my side work's done and Leeanne comes in, if she can get off from her other job on time and her baby-sitter's not late. You're gettin' expenses, you said. You can buy a tired lady some dinner and I'll tell you anything I can about that poor child."

6

The open-air Denny's above the ABC Store at the corner of Kalakaua and Kapahulu is without question the best location in the chain. The food's identical to all the others but the atmosphere is definitely above the standard. Louise and I found a table in the bar, away from the distractions of the nonstop beach party below. Louise ordered a Grand Slam and I had coffee.

"Mary MacGruder first came to work for us about two years ago. She was almost too young to serve drinks, and she had that look of, I don't know, she was unspoiled, I guess would be the word."

"Unspoiled."

"Virginal. You know, like a guy wouldn't want to *admit* to her that he drank alcohol, you know what I'm sayin'?"

"She was too young."

"That's not it. She was young, Lord knows. Young, blond and sweet. There was a feeling of grace about her. That's it! She looked like Grace Kelly used to, when she was makin' pictures, and she acted like a princess. For a while, some of the girls called her that—Princess—until she got mad and made them stop. Her name was Mary, she said, and she insisted that people call her by her name." Louise's dinner arrived. "Hungry," she said, and started eating. She was the kind of woman who could eat and talk at the same time and she wouldn't miss a crumb or a syllable.

"Mary could be quite strong when she wanted to be, hard even. Not at all the shy type. But she looked fragile. It fooled a lot of people. Anyway, none of us believed what happened to her. I mean, there just wasn't any way to know."

"It was a bad way to die."

"That's not it. You don't know, do you?"

"I guess not."

"She got fired. The company had a surprise drug test and her sample came up positive for cocaine. We're not supposed to know, but there are no real secrets around the hotel, you know."

"When was that?"

"About a year ago. It shocked all of us."

"Did you talk to her about it?"

"I'm not . . . I wasn't her boss. We were even on different shifts then, so I didn't see her all the time and when I did it was just a 'Hi, how are you?' kind of thing."

"What else did you hear?"

"Nothing. One day she was there and another—Bam! Out of there! When that happens, people talk in whispers about it and then they stop talking about it altogether."

"Did she have any family, any friends around?"

"Didn't see any when I worked with her."

"And you never saw her again?"

"I saw her a couple of times. She came in once, about three months after they fired her. She and another girl and a big fella, not local, but real, real big. Bigger than you. Taller, broader. White teeth. Rich guy, spent money by the bushel. And Mary and this other girl were hanging all over him.

"You know, it looked like they came in to just rub it in our faces. It was like she could come back any time she wanted and we couldn't do anything about it. She really acted the princess that night—treated us all like we were peasants. And a couple of the girls saw it, too, the way Mary and this big guy touched the other girl like she was some kind of a plaything. Like she wasn't real."

"What did the girl look like?"

"Young. Younger than Mary. Not bright, but pretty. And either drunk or stoned."

"And Mary and . . ."

"Somebody told me he was her boyfriend, but nobody knew his name. Don't remember who told me. Big, big guy, like I said. Huge shoulders. Lifts weights. A freak."

"You said you saw her one other time."

"I live on the North Shore. I was on the way to my dentist in Pearl Ridge and I stopped in Haleiwa for a shave ice. Mary was alone. She looked bad. Dirty, like she hadn't changed her clothes in a week. Dirty, matted hair, crud under her fingernails. She didn't recognize me and I almost didn't recognize her."

"When was this?"

"Three or four months ago. About then."

"She was killed three months ago."

"It was longer than that. Look, I felt sorry for her but I got my shave ice and went to see the dentist. Looked like her boyfriend kicked her out and she didn't know where to go. She might have been sleeping in the streets. But she wasn't my problem and I had other things to do. I didn't have anything against the girl. But she'd made her decisions, and she paid the price, I guess."

"It was a pretty steep price to pay," I said, remembering the photographs.

"I suppose it was, her bein' so young and all. I tell you, Mr. Caine, I've never seen a body go downhill as fast as that poor child did. When I first met her she was like some kind of a dream child, like the blue fairy in *The Wizard of Oz*, all sweet and innocent and beautiful. And the last time I saw her she looked kind of crazed and evil. To tell you the truth I didn't want to have anything to do with her. She scared me."

I nodded. What else was there to say?

"So you're workin' for the family. Guess they fired the other fella."

"What other fella?"

"About a month ago, when the police didn't seem to be coming up with anything, a private detective came around, said he was working for the girl's father. He some kind of army officer?"

"Some kind of officer," I said.

"This guy, he went to Human Resources, just like the police did, and they wouldn't tell him a thing. Not without a court order, or so I was told."

There wasn't anything about her being fired for drugs in the police file I read. "Did the police know about the drug thing?"

"How should I know what the police know? But I kind of doubt it. HR won't hold on to something like that if the employee doesn't sue, you know what I mean? They don't want to get sued by anybody for anything, so they keep that in the file only as long as they think the fired employee has a chance to complain or sue the company, and then they deep-six it so it doesn't leak and the employee can sue the company for tellin' on him. That make any sense to you?"

"It makes a lot of sense." I knew something the police didn't know. And it didn't get me anywhere, either. "Do you know the name of the other detective?"

"I'm good with names, sugar. Gotta be in my profession. But I don't think anybody ever told me. He was a local boy. Looked *hapa* Portagee to me. I never spoke with him, and he wasn't interested in talking with the help. But he was a local boy, just like I said. If he's in the book, he's bound to have a name that ends in an A."

7

I parked in a dirt lot on the eastern edge of Chinatown and nodded to the attendant leaning against the stone wall of an adjacent building. Chawlie would be waiting for me, even though it wasn't yet midnight. His intelligence network would have reported my arrival long before I walked the three short blocks to the restaurant he used as his headquarters.

Chawlie wasn't in his normal place and the plastic chairs in front of the restaurant were vacant. A soft young man in a dark suit and tie and a white-on-white dress shirt stood more or less at attention, watching my approach. His smile was uncertain, reminding me of a politician three weeks from election and ten points down on the polls.

"Mr. Caine! So good to see you tonight!" He pumped my hand vigorously. "I am Mr. Choy. How are you feeling?" His English was California Standard. I guessed Stanford or Berkeley.

"Nobody shot me."

"I am certain Uncle will be happy to hear that," said Mr. Choy, his smile strained. "Please come this way. Uncle is waiting for you."

He led me across the bright dining area to a pair of carved mahogany doors. The doors and the frame formed the top nine tenths of a circle, finished in a dark stain that contrasted with the otherwise brightly painted and lighted restaurant.

"Please enter, Mr. Caine," said Choy, extending his left hand toward the portal in the fashion of the best hotelier, his head inclined in a neat little bow that could have been either cultural or the result of training in his profession. I entered a darkened room and stood in the doorway to allow my pupils time to adjust.

"So. Nobody shoot you. That is good. And you are early to pay a debt. That too is good! Come and sit." Chawlie was sitting behind a low table attended by two young women, one of whom was my visitor of the previous night. She had the same haughty look she sported aboard *Duchess*. The other girl kept her eyes down, demurely avoiding my gaze as I crammed my legs under the table.

"You are an honorable man, John Caine."

"We had a contract," I said, reaching into my backpack for the money. Chawlie held up his hand.

"A mere favor," said Chawlie. "It isn't necessary to pay me yet." Knowing Chawlie, I began to comprehend that this conversation would take me places I hadn't planned on going.

"I thought about the favor you asked of me," he continued. "Instead of cash payment I would like a small favor from you."

"You know I will do anything within reason for an old friend," I replied, understanding an offer when I heard one. Other thoughts flashed through my mind in rapid succession, one following another in an undeniable progression: *Chawlie had kept a copy of the file. And he had read it. And he had found something of interest.* Possibilities swarmed.

"There is a man mentioned in the police file," said Chawlie. "This man I would like to know about."

I nodded, waiting for what would follow. If Chawlie wanted me to commit myself on anything he was to be disappointed.

"This man. His name is Thompson."

It clicked. Carter Allen Thompson was the name of Mary

MacGruder's former boyfriend, the owner of the last address she claimed. He had been interviewed by the police and told them he hadn't seen her for some time, that she had lived with him, but moved out a month before, leaving him no clue to where she'd gone. It was Thompson who provided the first hint of drug abuse. He was already on my call list, and after talking to Louise I wanted to know more about him.

"What is it you wish to know about Mr. Thompson?"

"Thompson and I had business dealings in the past. They were not satisfactory." Chawlie rose from the table, carefully disentangling himself from his two attendants. "Walk with me to the river."

Chawlie's girls remained behind and we left the restaurant through a side door to a narrow alley. I followed him through the passageway to the broad promenade beside the Nu'uanu Stream. Chawlie stopped in the shadow of Sun Yat-sen's statue.

"Thompson is not to be trusted. He will tell you one thing, but do not believe him. Look for the lies. *Acch! Pit!*" Chawlie spat toward the river into the darkness, oblivious to the passing pedestrian traffic.

"What do you want to know, Uncle?"

"I have a son, a good boy. Thompson claims he owes him money. Garrick likes to gamble. He is not skilled. He likes girls, too, but not the ones I can get him. It has become a problem. He now has tastes I cannot provide."

I frowned. I did not need another client. Especially one for free. I had enough of those at the moment.

"The boy would not come to me, I learn this from friends. I find this out two days ago and wonder what to do. I think of you and then you come to me with your request. I think, This John Caine, he might be the answer. So I get you police file and find the answer there."

"Thompson is into gambling?"

"Among other things."

"Like what?"

Chawlie hocked again and lofted another gob into the night. I've spent a good portion of my adult life in Asia, but I'd never accustomed myself to the habit. I'd heard somewhere that the Chinese spit to rid themselves of evil spirits. If that was the case, the mention of Carter Allen Thompson's name brought the evil spirits with it.

"Videos," said Chawlie, so quietly I nearly missed it.

"I beg your pardon?"

"Mr. Thompson makes videos and sells them to Japan and Taiwan. Some to Hong Kong. Mostly Japan. Always blondes."

My brain finally caught up. For a moment I had pictured stacks of pirated copies of *Dumbo* and *Dances with Wolves*. Now I understood. Blondes in Asia are as valuable as the gold their hair resembles. Natural blondes are considered the crème de la crème. Japan, Hong Kong and Taiwan all had enough males in their thirties and forties with enough disposable income to indulge their fantasies in that specific kind of pornography. Thompson had taken a specialty market and refined it.

"He is Australian. Had trouble at home and can't go back," continued Chawlie, his voice soft. I could hear the antagonism. "He is not here with all the proper papers. But he thinks he is big businessman."

"Where can I find him?"

"Pacific Tower on Bishop Street. Thirtieth floor."

"Impressive address," I said.

Chawlie grunted. To a man who owned entire blocks of downtown Honolulu, a man who merely rented one floor of a high-rise was of no consequence.

"What would you like to know about him?"

"Find out where he gambles, where he has his games. My son will not tell me."

"You have no other way to find out?"

Chawlie smiled. "Jasmine, my young woman, the one you met last night. She works for him. Receptionist at his movie production office. Most trusted employee. She will help you."

"Why me?"

"Use your head, John Caine. I help you, you help me. Best to get Garrick out of Islands before it is too late. I have him locked up now, but can't keep him there forever. I can handle this Thompson, but need to know more about him first. You do that for me."

"Put your son on a plane."

"It is worse than that."

I understood. Chawlie's son had been threatened by Thompson and Chawlie was frightened for him. It must have been a shock to find his son hooked on the same vices he purveyed to others.

"What else is Thompson into, besides gambling and pornography?"

"Drugs, girls, guns, movies. Everything people want." It occurred to me that Chawlie himself might be just a little afraid of the man. "He has entertainment company, construction company, fishing boats."

"Do the police know about this man?"

Chawlie spat once again. "If police know anything, you think they would know where to look? Or you think they have their hands where their hands should not be?" He let that hang between us before continuing. "Besides, if police try to get into his business, he smell them right away. But you different."

"Me? How am I different?"

Chawlie laughed and spat another time past the statue of Sun Yat-sen. "He smell a cop. He also smell another crook. He smell you he think, Hell, you no cop. You a crook!"

VVVVVVVV

8

*D*uchess wallowed in a slight chop, a stray trade wind ruffling the calm surface of Pearl Harbor, the breeze banging the rigging against the wooden mast. I checked the lines and went below. *Duchess* is all wood. There's no fiberglass, no aluminum, no plastic on her. She is not a Tupperware boat. In a deliberate contravention of the notion that lighter is better, she has the only wooden stick in the marina. She's an anachronism, like her owner.

Duchess contains everything I own. She has complete stores of food and full tanks of water and diesel. To leave in a hurry it would only be necessary to slip the dock lines and motor out of the channel. I'm a confirmed nomad and I like it that way.

Like water, food and fuel, I keep all my cash on board, a fact no one is privy to. I removed the five thousand dollars from my backpack and went forward to the chain locker. Inside, at the forward peak behind a false panel in the bulkheads, is my bank. There was nearly two hundred thousand dollars in hundreds and fifties stored there in neat, banded piles. My retirement fund. It's a big space, and the stacks of bills looked small, considering what they would buy.

Short term, the money would purchase a lot of shiny, pretty toys, but for the long term it wouldn't buy much. I needed at least five times that amount before I was satisfied. I didn't want to spend my declining years scrambling for enough change to buy dog food. And that is a vast improvement over the ideas of the future I'd previously held. There had been a time when retirement was not a consideration. The possibility of living that long never crossed my mind. From an actuarial standpoint I'd exceeded my life expectancy several times and I'd lived my life accordingly.

I felt ragged from too little sleep, too much alcohol and caffeine and too much pointless conversation. Chawlie's request was an unwelcome burden and took me out of focus, whether Thompson had anything to do with Mary MacGruder's death or not. The fight with the two local boys depressed me. My shoulder hurt. I didn't know where to go or what to do next and I was almost too tired to care.

A warm shower relaxed me and I headed to my bunk in the forward cabin. Something about the air disturbed me, the humidity insinuating itself around every inch of flesh the way it does when a hurricane is near.

It didn't have to be a hurricane. What I'd learned about Mary MacGruder was making my skin crawl of its own accord. I pulled the *Atlas of Asia* down from the bookshelves that lined my bunk and opened it to my favorite passage. Nestled inside a cutout was my Colt .45 1911A Gold Cup automatic pistol. I checked the load and slipped it under my pillow before I crawled naked between the percale.

I awoke the next morning full of purpose. Since everything seemed to be a dead end and I still didn't have anything to take to the police I decided to find the private investigator who had visited the hotel, and see where that would take me.

The yellow pages had only one private investigator whose name ended in A. Robert W. Souza had an address listed in Waikiki, beneath the western flank of Diamond Head. It wasn't an impressive location. Behind the glitz and glitter of the thirty-story hotels along the beach, Waikiki is the home of the worst urban slums on the island. The streets are narrow, the apartments filled to overflowing. Crime is an everyday occurrence. The predators prey on the tourists and on each other. Along McCulley Avenue the iteration of the food chain is out in the open.

Parking is another problem. There isn't any. And due to the high crime rate there are police everywhere. They don't put a dent in the crime rate, but they do notice illegal parking. The Honolulu PD doesn't write parking tickets, it tows your car. I didn't want to pay the mandatory two-hundred-dollar fine for towing so I searched for a legal parking spot, got lucky and found one two blocks away.

The morning sun had neared its zenith and was blazing on my back as I trotted along. By the time I reached the detective's office sweat was pouring down the back of my shirt and dripping into my eyes.

The building was a small strip center with storefront businesses and enough parking for only the tenants. A Chinese CPA had the space nearest the street, a hair salon and an upholstery shop occupied the next two. Unit D, the address listed in the yellow pages for Robert W. Souza, Private Investigator, was vacant.

The door was locked so I peered through the glass. The office wore the shabby look of a place that had been unoccupied for weeks. There was no furniture. A white telephone rested on its side, the handset flung against the dark, soiled carpet like a broken arm. Letters, newspapers and business cards were piled beneath the mail slot. The one envelope I could read through the glass was addressed to Souza.

I went to the CPA's office. The interior was shaded from the morning sun by miniblinds and chilled by powerful air conditioning. It was so cool my back felt cold immediately. I stood in a small waiting room that was dominated by an unoccupied secretary's desk. There was a sign that said w. WONG, CPA over a blue door.

I noticed a bell on the desk, the kind you hit with your palm. I touched it gently. The bell produced a ring that carried a nostalgic trace of childhood school days with it. A man came out of the back room. He was of average height with a slender build. He had coal black hair and a thin mustache.

"Hello?" he said. There was some caution in his manner, as if he expected violence.

"I'm looking for Robert Souza," I said. "I thought his office was here."

"Unit D, yah?"

"Yes. Robert Souza, the private detective."

"I understand he moved out about a month ago."

"Did he leave a forwarding address?"

"No. Not that I know of. Why don't you contact the leasing agent?"

"Do you have his name?"

"Yah. Let me check. Wait here, please." He held out his hand, palm down, as if warding off my advance.

He disappeared behind the blue door again and closed it behind him. I heard the lock click shut. I waited a full five minutes before he returned.

"Her name is Nagada. Laurie Nagada. Here's her telephone number." He handed me one of his cards with the name and number of the leasing agent scrawled across the back.

"Thank you," I said.

He went back through the blue door and closed it without acknowledgment.

I let myself out.

Back out in the heat I took my cellular phone from my pack and tried the number. It was busy. I walked back to my parking space, hitting send over and over again, trying to get through. Her line was busy until after I'd found my Jeep, stowed the backpack away and pulled out into traffic. On impulse I tried it again. It rang.

I shifted the phone to my left shoulder as I steered and shifted my way through heavy traffic on McCulley while I waited for Ms. Nagada to answer. When she did she sounded harried.

"Hello?" Her voice was on the edge of hysteria.

"Hello, Ms. Nagada? My name is Caine. John Caine. I'm looking for—"

"I'm not interested," she said. "And it's Miss Nagada."

"I'm not selling and I'm sorry about the 'Miss.' "

"So am I, brother. What did you say your name was? What's that noise in the background? Are you on a car phone?"

"Sort of. My name is John Caine and I'm looking for one of your tenants, Robert Souza. He used to be at—"

"Old Magnum PI. I know where he used to be, that asshole. He left in the middle of the night. Took all his stuff and just moved out. He left owing, too. All that damage to the place, his deposit didn't even begin to cover it."

"Do you know where he went?"

"I can't find him. It's possible he left the island."

"Certified letters with return receipt requested?"

"No forwarding address. And the other tenants are going crazy because strange people keep stopping by looking for this character."

"I understand. Mr. Wong gave me your name and number."

"Then you must be nice. He runs most of them off."

"What kind of damage to his place?"

"Oh, you know. Papers strewn all over, holes in the walls and ceilings. Holes kicked in the doors. The medicine cabinet on the bathroom floor. There was even a hole in the ceiling big enough to crawl up to the attic space. Why he'd do that is beyond me, too. But who can figure? That's the last time I'll rent to a private eye."

What she'd described was a thoroughly professional search.

"When did this happen?"

"About a month ago. Right when he disappeared. He didn't pay his rent and I went around to collect or post the notice and I found his office that way. It's been vacant ever since."

I thanked Miss Nagada and hit the End button. Someone had moved Mr. Souza out. All the way out. Someone had also gone through his office, including the walls and ceilings, and they hadn't wasted any time doing so. I made a bet with myself that Mr. Souza was feeding the fish somewhere offshore.

I called information and got a residential listing for a Souza, Robert W. The prefix was for Makiki, an old section of town not far from Waikiki and even more run-down. I phoned the number given and was told by the recorded message that it was disconnected and no longer in service.

If it was listed, the address would be in the directory. I spotted a phone booth with a directory hanging below on a chain and pulled in beside it. I found his address. It was on Young Street, near the old police station. I knew the area well. Souza's place was within three blocks of the phone booth. I decided to walk.

His apartment was on the third floor of a concrete-block building that looked as if it might survive a hundred hurricanes. It had all the charm and architectural appeal of a bomb shelter. There was a small hand-lettered sign that said the manager was in the back apartment, second floor, no vacancy. I went up a set of concrete steps and found her.

She was an ancient, bent Japanese woman wrapped in layers of sweaters despite the midsummer heat, the kind of wonderful, revered creature the Hawaiians call *kapuna*. Her brown, wizened face peered up at me through thick lenses, making me think of an apple left too long in the sun. She wore a quizzical expression.

"Hello?" Her voice was tremulous and uncertain.

"Hello, Auntie," I said, dropping into the Islander's habit of referring to any woman over sixty. "I am looking for one of your tenants. Mr. Souza?"

A curious calm came over her and she straightened, staring at me through the clear lenses of her glasses, her eyes magnified to twice their normal size. Her gaze was intense.

"He is dead," she declared.

"I'm sorry." It was all I could think of to say. Her response had not been one I'd anticipated.

"He kill himself, they say, but I know different. They come for him, that's why. In the middle of the night. Two men. They knock on his door. He let them in. They go inside. Hour later, they go out. Next morning, he dead."

Wondering at her narrative, I nodded.

"They say he call police and tell them he going to kill himself. And that he did. Overdose of da kine drug. Bad 'ting, that. He leave a note. They say he kill himself. Two men, they kill him. They did it and blame him, that's why."

"Who said he killed himself?"

"The police. I tell them what I saw. They don't believe me. I'm an old woman, but I watch. I don't sleep. So I watch. I know my building."

"How long ago was this?"

"One month. Just before rent due."

"Have you rented the apartment?"

She shook her head. "He leave big mess. Police make even bigger mess. Have to paint, that's why. Move out his stuff. It takes me long time to paint da kine apartment. My fingers hurt, that's why."

"May I see the apartment?"

She studied me again, her scrutiny extending from the top of my haole head to my sandaled feet. I was dressed as a local in shorts and T-shirt. "I give you key, you bring it back?"

"Of course, Auntie."

She went inside and brought out a ring of brass keys that must have weighed ten pounds. "This here every key. His was

eight, on top floor in the back. I can't see that key but it's here."
She handed me the cluster of keys, the means of entry to every
door in the building.

"You bring it back, you hear?"

"I will, Auntie," I said. I had not even told her why I wanted
to find Souza. This lady remembered Hawaii as it used to be.

The third floor was a repetition of the second. Eight was in
the back, concrete block walls interrupted only by a window
and a door. I found a key with "8" stamped in the brass and
tried it.

The door opened out. A musty emanation, the lingering
scent of a protective ghost, came out to greet me along with a
blast of superheated air. I stepped inside and looked around in
the gloom. Curtains were drawn on every window. A tiny
kitchen, little more than an extension of the entry, was to the
right of the door, a bedroom and a bath on the left. The living
room was directly in front of me. I flicked a switch. No light
came on.

I left the door open for both light and air and started across
the room. I banged my knee painfully on a file drawer that was
pulled out of a metal cabinet against the wall. I closed the
drawer and started across the room again, this time with greater
caution. Piles of manila file folders and reports were tossed
carelessly on the furniture and the floor. I opened the sliding
glass door that led to a tiny lanai and pulled the curtains back.
Now I could see. In a little while I hoped to be able to breathe.

It didn't take long to see that whoever encouraged the late
Robert Souza to shuffle off this mortal coil had also gone
through everything the same way they did in his office. My
guess was that they came here first, then took his keys to his
office and ransacked that place. The police wouldn't have made
this kind of a mess. It was as if someone had intentionally done
this. It was like spitting on a grave.

It began to look as though Souza had found something he
should not have found. If he had anything solid about Mary

MacGruder's murder, someone had beaten me to it. By about a month. I didn't expect to find anything now. The trail was cold. Souza wouldn't have expected any trouble resulting from that case. It was pretty straightforward. If he had, would he have hidden whatever it was that he found out? Would he have understood its value? And would they have found whatever it was they were looking for? Whoever *they* were.

There wasn't any reason to look through the files on the floor. Everything that could be learned had already left this sad place.

I closed the sliding glass door and the curtains and locked the entry door again. I returned the keys to the little *kapuna* downstairs and walked back to my Jeep. On impulse I called Katherine Alapai, the lead investigator on the case, and got lucky. She agreed to meet me in twenty minutes.

VVVVVVVV

9

Detective Alapai suggested we meet at Kelly's, a locals-only, twenty-four-hour coffee shop on Nimitz Highway near the airport. Kelly's is fluorescent bright, always open and anonymous. Visibility is high. I gathered she wanted to meet there because it was safe.

She'd demanded that I describe myself, including what I was wearing and what I was driving, so when I parked the Jeep in Kelly's lot I understood that my movements would be watched. No one accosted me as I entered the restaurant, looking for the detective. She had not described herself.

"Mr. Caine?"

A big hand gripped me and a beefy, middle-aged local crowded me from behind, violating my space. He pinioned my shoulder with one hand and expertly frisked me with the other. Satisfied, he backed away and smiled.

"I'm Lieutenant Kahanamoku, Honolulu PD. What's in the pack, bruddah?"

"Take a look." I shrugged it off my shoulder and handed it to him.

"Why not?" He unzipped the compartments and looked through them, finding my bandanna and a copy of Michael Crichton's latest paperback and not much else. The cop sniffed at my cellular telephone and my knife, a Buck Folding Hunter, and tossed them back. "No firearms?"

"Now why would I do that?"

He smiled and handed the bag back. "Some people just don't have da good sense God geeve 'em, Mr. Caine. Come on. She's in here."

He led me past the counter to the last booth against the back wall. A small woman with lustrous black hair and pale skin watched me. She would have been beautiful but for a hard shell around her that she wore like armor, visible to anyone who cared to look deep enough. She nodded, acknowledging my presence. The big cop took up residence at a table out of earshot, but continued watching me like a pit bull on point.

"Detective Alapai?"

"Have a seat, Mr. Caine. I ordered you coffee, courtesy of the City and County of Honolulu. You want anything else you'll have to pay for it yourself."

"Coffee's fine."

"Do you have some identification?" I handed over my Hawaii driver's license. She glanced at it and tossed it back. She already knew who I was. That's why I was frisked coming into the restaurant. "Okay, you're a citizen. You called me. What do you want?"

"I'm looking into the death of Mary MacGruder. I understand you are the detective in charge of the investigation."

Detective Alapai stared at me through fathomless black eyes. She seemed to say, So what? She continued to look at me, waiting for my next statement.

"There is no suspect in the case?"

"No." A flat statement, unembellished by facial movements or other body language.

"There is some information you may not have. I wanted to share it with you."

"Who are you working for, Mr. Caine?"

"Her father, Vice Admiral Winston MacGruder III, is my former commanding officer. It is his interests I'm most concerned with."

"You are a licensed private investigator?"

"I've got a license."

"Who's your client here?"

"I'm a friend of the family."

She frowned. She knew she couldn't go further than that. Licensed private investigators have nearly the same privacy privileges as attorneys in this state.

"You seem to have turned up in our files before. The last time was about three months ago."

"The Greek dope thing, you mean?"

She nodded. "You were shot during that 'Greek dope thing.' What was it? Bounty hunting?"

"Nothing so glamorous, Detective. I got in their way and they got in mine. DEA's got a file."

"I've read it," she said. "And I read your life history, according to what they faxed over. I found it fascinating how a federal agency could get tied up with someone like you. But you didn't answer my question. What exactly do you do for a living?"

"I'm a licensed private eye, but mostly I do protective services. I'm also a diving instructor. That's on my tax return. Mainly I do favors for friends. Think of me as a retriever."

"It makes you sound like a big dog, Mr. Caine, which you are not. Dogs are friendly. Dogs are helpful. Dogs are obedient. Why do I get the feeling you are none of the above? And what are you doing messing around in my homicide investigation?"

"Same thing you are. Trying to find the killers."

She flinched. "What makes you think there was more than one?"

"At least two. And I'd bet on a van. I looked at the Shark Cave yesterday. That's pretty deserted country up there, but cars pass by at decent intervals. Dumping a body looks like dumping a body, nothing else. If the person didn't want to be caught he'd need help."

"You've read the file." It was an accusation.

"I have." I didn't want to be caught in a lie with this woman.

"The complete file? Photos? Field notes? Everything?"

I nodded.

"Shit."

The consequences of a police file copied and sold to a civilian were immense. I would not have volunteered that I had seen the file, but she'd asked. She got it out into the open like a dog going for a bone. This detective was good. And she was dangerous.

"Where did you get the idea about the van?"

I explained my hypothesis, postulated while walking the site.

"If you've seen the file, then you have everything we do."

"Maybe something you don't." And I told her about the private investigator who had died in Makiki, and how it looked like a related homicide. "He was working on this case, following up your own investigation, and he crossed the wrong path. Someone canceled him out."

"What else do you have?"

"Souza's apartment was thoroughly searched. So was his office. They even kicked holes in the walls and cut a hole in the ceiling a man could crawl through. I'm willing to bet both events took place on the same night. I'd also give you odds that the keys to his office were not among the items inventoried on his person."

She nodded, thinking. "Okay, I'll buy that. Anything else?"

For some reason the name of Mary's landlord popped into my mind and a little voice told me to keep it to myself. If Chawlie had a reason to find Thompson interesting, and if Thompson was involved in this case in even a small way, it might be counterproductive to even hint to the police about him. The information I'd gleaned from the waitress was mere gossip and it was unflattering to Mary's memory and therefore dangerous to the admiral.

"Not much. I've just been on this for a few days."

"Do you want to tell me where you got the file now, or should I arrest you and have you explain it to my captain?"

"I'll take my chances with the captain, Detective."

Anger smoldered behind anthracite eyes. I could see the steel in them. It was not something I wanted to challenge lightly. "You have no right to a police file, Mr. Caine. Your status won't protect you. Right now you have admitted at least two felonies to a sworn police officer, and further incriminated yourself by admitting you have read the file. I could get a warrant for your arrest based on that information. So why don't you make it easier on everyone and tell me where you got it."

"Okay. Two nights ago a young woman, whose name I don't know except as Jasmine, came to my boat and gave me the file. I suspect Jasmine is not her real name and I had never seen her before nor do I expect to see her again." I left out the fact that I'd seen her since, hoping Alapai would not ask that question.

"You expect me to believe that?"

"It's the truth."

"Jasmine. I can assume that's her *nom de whore?*"

"I have no idea."

She nodded. "And I suppose you'll tell me that you no longer have that file in your possession, that if we get a warrant we won't find it no matter how hard we look, so if you keep quiet we won't have grounds to hold you. Is that right?"

"That's about it, Detective."

"You're cute, all right. And you're probably right. Okay. Suppose we buy your story about the investigator. How did you come to that conclusion?"

I told her about my footwork, working through the cocktail waitresses in Waikiki, learning that both the police and the other private investigator had contacted Human Resources and did not bother talking with the current employees as Mary had not been employed there for over a year.

"We'll interview the manager again. You've got some good moves, Mr. Caine." She looked at me, appraising me as if for the first time. "Maybe you're not the clown I thought you were. Maybe DEA was right."

"What did they say about me?"

"Only that you could be trusted to do the right thing unless your personal interests conflicted with ours. Is that what you're going to do on this? Are you going to screw up my investigation?"

"Not if I can help it."

"But you might."

"If I can't help it."

She smiled, and I saw the beautiful woman behind the hard, professional mask. "We might be able to work together on this, but I won't give you anything. You come to me and tell me what you've got. You want to cooperate with me it's going to be all one-sided. I've got stuff nobody else does and I'm not sharing it with anybody, especially an outsider. If you give me what you find, I'll confirm it. But I won't feed you what I already have. Do you understand?"

I nodded, sensing an offer coming. The conditions were not unexpected.

"It has to be this way. You've already given me several things to think about. The file was lifted and copied and sold and Jasmine or whoever gave it to you. That can't happen; there are procedures in place that make that impossible. But you say it happened, okay, it happened. I'm going to sit on that right now. I like your idea about the van. It makes sense and it ties into something else I already know.

"And you're going to ruin one detective's day when I suggest that he look into a closed suicide case that might be a homicide connected to one I'm working. I'll keep your name out of that, too. Otherwise you'll have an enemy you don't need.

"So I like the idea of you being out there, working this. You might uncover something I can't."

"I go blindly floundering about, stirring up the dust. If I get in trouble I'm on my own, but if I get lucky you get the credit."

She grinned, showing perfect white teeth. It lowered the armor momentarily, making her look like a little girl. "You've got the picture."

"Aren't you going to give me a place to start?"

I could almost hear wheels and gears whirring inside her head while she considered it. I sipped my coffee and kept my mouth shut. I'd known her all of ten minutes and already I knew that any appeal would result in a negative.

"A father naturally wants to believe the best of his daughter. You want to know what really happened? Does the admiral?"

I nodded.

"It's pretty brutal stuff."

"The world's a pretty brutal place," I told her. "It could break your heart."

"Spare me the sarcasm," she said. "It doesn't add anything to this conversation and if you shut up you might learn something."

I shut up. There's a time to argue and there's a time to keep your mouth closed.

"The file isn't everything we have, you know that. The daughter was connected to some players that scare me shitless."

"Drugs?"

"I only wish it were that simple."

This woman was not the kind of person to admit fear of anything or anyone. Of the two cops in the restaurant, she was the most dangerous.

"For the last year of her life she lived with a man in Haleiwa," she said. "Too bad you no longer have the file. His name's in there. If you had it and were good you'd see what I saw. Be cautious. He's connected to some really bad people. I want you to form your own conclusions and then filter them through me. It'll be a check system. I'll be your only contact. I know you know others on HPD, but this one's mine. Only mine. Understand?"

I nodded.

"Say it, Mr. Caine."

"I understand."

"Oh, by the way. You said you were out at the Shark Cave yesterday. You didn't run into a couple of local boys out there, did you?"

"Local boys?"

"The report we got was that they were minding their own business when a man matching your description went berserk and beat the hell out of them. You wouldn't know anything about any of that, would you?"

"No, ma'am."

"I didn't think so."

"They didn't have records of arrests and convictions, did they? These local boys?"

"You mean, did they have a history of car theft? Stuff like that?"

"Yeah. Stuff like that."

"They have arrest records that go back to the fourth grade. And yes, they specialized in stolen cars. Are you psychic, Mr. Caine?"

"Just a lucky guess, Detective Alapai," I said.

VYYYYYYY

10

I left the coffee shop and drove directly back to the marina. From what I'd learned the file warranted another reading.

The sun fell behind the Waianae Mountains as I headed home, a bright glare shining directly into the eyes. Smoky haze hovered over the far cane fields as the harvest continued. In a few years the final curtain will be dropped on the plantation era in Hawaii. Lanai shut down its pineapple fields a few years ago, that quiet island converting to expensive hotels, golf courses and luxury homes. Every year Oahu loses more and more agricultural acreage to suburbia, while Dole and C&H flee to the cheap land and cheaper labor of the Philippines, far away from labor unions, EPA and OSHA.

I'm not lamenting a lost way of life. From what I understand the plantation existence was not a good one. But transitions are always hard on those going through them. Displacement is never agreeable. Hawaii will be forever changed. But then it has changed every year since Captain Cook saw mountain peaks rising over the horizon and thought he'd better take a look. I'd like to think we've made improvements, but that lie is exposed each time I anchor *Duchess* in a pristine cove where development has yet to reach, where coconut palms line pristine white beaches and the only sound is the gentle roaring of the distant surf far out on the reef.

I found a parking place close to the dock and unlocked my boat. Her electronic detection system told me *Duchess* had been undisturbed during my absence. I went below and retrieved the file from its hiding place and set up a bank of cushions on the aft deck against the cabin facing the sun. An opened bottle of Kendall-Jackson provided me with a chilled glass of chardonnay. I set up the file and read through it again, sipping the wine and letting the Kona winds riffle my hair. Pearl Harbor's surface was luminous from the slanting rays of the sun.

Finding another body in this mess was an unpleasant surprise. There were questions, too, about the people I was stalking, but they had to slide for the moment. I didn't yet know enough to know what those questions were, let alone know how to answer them. I contented myself with the file.

Detective Alapai had mentioned the man Mary MacGruder lived with in Haleiwa. She'd hinted he might be the starting point for my search, and that she knew something she wanted me to confirm. But I'd come across him before. He'd been in the file and in my conversation with the cocktail waitress, and from Chawlie. Thompson was almost certainly the man Louise had seen with Mary and the other girl. A big man, she had said. Bigger than me. Broader. A freak.

Katherine Alapai knew something I didn't and she wanted independent corroboration. Chawlie wanted information about him, too, and had sent his little woman-toy Jasmine to become a spy in the enemy camp. He'd also recruited me. Did Chawlie know something about Thompson that he wasn't telling me? Of course. That was Chawlie's style. Even if it were easier to be direct, Chawlie would take the interesting course.

All lines of logical progression crossed at Thompson. It wasn't a stretch to conclude that he had something to do with Mary's murder and possibly something to do with Souza's. I needed an approach. Everyone has a vulnerability, a handle to use to get to them. Once I found that, access was easy. Even the president of the United States will pick up the telephone if you have the right number. It all comes down to information. Finding that handle would be easier if the guy was dirty, and both Chawlie and Katherine Alapai were sure that he was.

What was a girl that reminded people of Princess Grace doing living with a man like Thompson? People attract for the strangest of reasons, but this pairing made Fay Wray and King Kong seem like Ozzie and Harriet. What had Mary MacGruder been getting out of this man? Drugs? I'd heard of coke whores before who'd sell their bodies and their souls for the white powder and there was evidence that she might have had a problem with the stuff. Sex? With the face and figure she possessed she could have had any man, if it were only a man she wanted.

I reminded myself why I was involved. Max had given me this mission to find her murderer and to protect her father. I'd become so focused in tracking down her killers I'd nearly overlooked the fact that protecting her reputation, and her father's, was the more important of the two goals. There were some nasty stories floating around about her but she was dead, a murder victim, and those stories would taper off in time unless there was some hard evidence to back them up, or unless they surfaced again in a murder trial. That's what I was afraid I'd find at the end of the trail. That is what Max feared when he'd handed me this quest.

The best way to find out seemed to be through Thompson.

There was little data in the police notes about the man. There was just his name and a short statement he'd given the police, saying he had not seen Mary for a month, that he did not monitor her whereabouts. Other than his short statement there were few facts about him. He listed his occupation as an entertainment producer. That could mean anything from a producer of feature-length motion pictures to a street-hustling pimp.

Forensic evidence put another man at the scene, an Asian. My own conclusion was that more than one man had to be involved. Did Thompson have a partner? And if so, was he a left-handed, AB-positive Asian? Laughter bubbled from deep in my chest. All I needed now was a severe British fellow in a deer-stalker, waving his meerschaum, sagely telling me it was all quite elementary, my dear Caine.

This was beyond my experience. My training had been to plan and perform high-risk, high-reward operations using a small team of similarly trained specialists, each of us capable of extreme violence. Get in, get done and get out. Be gone before the smoke cleared and the dust settled. As a civilian my jobs tended to be similar but were more of a protective nature, preventing others from achieving what my own teams could have done. Imagine the worst scenario and plan for it. Protect the executive and his family from harm, make certain his stay in the Islands would be a pleasant one. With that kind of problem I was in my element. But in this arena I was the amateur, stalking the grizzled gladiator, armed only with my wooden sword.

I closed the file and locked it away again. I washed out the glass in the galley and put on my Nikes for my evening run.

This time I ran the bike path all the way to Pearl City. It's a ten-mile round trip from my slip in the marina to the Monkey Bar and back. The sun had already gone down when I returned. It was pitch black under the canopy of kiawe trees near the end of the run and I felt a little uneasy padding through there. If someone had ill feelings toward me this would be where they would have the best advantage. But this path was the only access to the base on foot. There was no way around it. Thinking that I was retracing Souza's path, I felt patches of ice from my neck to my shoulder blades. I increased my pace until I reached the well-lighted parking lot near the Marina Restaurant.

An empty *Duchess* welcomed me home, creaking a lonely tune through her rigging. I'd managed to convince myself that Thompson was somehow connected to Mary's murder and I was committed to finding the leverage to reach him, regardless of what it took.

After changing, I spent a quiet hour on deck smoking a Cuban Romeo y Julietta and thinking of a way to gain access, reflecting on what I'd learned about Thompson from Louise, from Katherine Alapai, and from Chawlie.

It took about that long to reach a decision. Sometimes the direct approach is the best one. In this case it looked like the only one.

11

At nine o'clock the next morning I was sitting at a side-walk cafe in the shadow of the Pacific Tower waiting for CAT Productions, Inc., to begin its business day. All I'd managed to deduce so far was that "CAT" was Carter Allen Thompson's initials.

I'd already visited CAT's floor twice and found the entire floor locked off the elevator. For the past twenty minutes I'd entertained myself in the open-air pastry shop with a morning paper, a cup of coffee and a bear claw. The paper told me things I didn't want to know about people for whom I cared little or nothing. Someone in the Middle East had done something unforgivable. Congress had done something unprintable. The president had done something unpardonable. A hurricane was thrashing Guam and a tropical storm was forming off the coast of South America, gaining strength as it pushed its way into the Pacific. It wasn't a problem yet, but it was causing concern to the local weather people who were paid to be concerned about such things.

I was dressed in my best Hawaiian business sincere, in a raw silk sport coat, a white Oxford-cloth shirt with an open collar and tropical-weight wool trousers. Both the jacket and the pants were natural colored, offsetting my deep-water tan. I carried an aluminum Haliburton briefcase. It was a prop designed to make me look like a successful businessman from Kahala. The briefcase was filled with Sunday's *Advertiser*.

By nine-thirty most of the office workers had been busy for over an hour. I'd read all there was to read in the paper and I didn't want another cup of coffee. I walked around the block, pausing outside the Honolulu Book Shop to look in the window. The new Stephen Hawking book seemed interesting and I went in for a sample read. By the time I'd made my purchase I decided it was time that even pornographers should be at their desks, beginning a busy day of photographing blondes with their legs open, or whatever they did that passed as work. I walked back to the elevator lobby on the harbor side of the building.

Two approaches to Thompson were possible. Neither was foolproof, but the first was the weaker. It had the advantage of not having to work for any length of time, just long enough to get me in the door. I wasn't worried about the receptionist, Chawlie's girl, who had been briefed, but I had to be in the presence of the man before I decided to try the second scheme.

The second scheme, the big con, had been approved by Chawlie. I'd gone back to Chinatown last night to seek his approval and advice. After I'd sketched out my approach, he offered refinements of his own.

Chawlie told me more about his son Garrick, the good boy who liked blondes and gambling but was not effective with either. This time he told me the truth—or part of the truth. I was never sure with Chawlie. Garrick had been working for Thompson until this week, when Chawlie's people swept him off the streets and got him into hiding. Now he wanted me to pretend to sell the boy to Thompson, to use him as a Judas goat to get Thompson out in the open. I thought Chawlie's plan risky, but he insisted. It was his son, after all, and he was confident he had the resources to protect him.

My first approach was my cover story to get in to see Thompson. I was Harold Jenkins, senior insurance adjuster for the Fidelity Casualty & Life Insurance Company of Seattle, and I was looking into the death of one Mary MacGruder. I was fussy, anal-retentive and committed to trivia. I was the bureaucrat personified. I even had a business card. Several of them. I expected Mr. Thompson to be suspicious of a cold call from Mr. Jenkins, but the receptionist would cover by calling the company and checking my bona fides. It's a real company and Mr. Jenkins is a highly regarded employee. I'd met him once and he gave me a handful of his cards, and for just this kind of occasion I decided to keep them.

Once in Thompson's presence I'd play it by ear. My aim was to get into his confidence. The police would have played it too cute, would have tried too hard to look like criminals to get inside. Once that lie is exposed, the rest of the charade would soon tumble. I decided to play it straight once I was inside his guard, abandon the little con for the bigger one.

Maybe Chawlie was right. Maybe I am a crook.

I rode an empty elevator nonstop to the thirtieth floor. This time the elevator doors opened into a reception room that could only be described as Japanese Modern Severe. Hardwood floors were offset by stark, nearly naked white walls. What little furniture there was was black lacquered enamel. Very chic. Very expensive. A teak and ebony wood representation of a black cat entwining itself around a pole dominated the far wall, CAT Productions' logo. I got it. The cat was acting sensually, the pole a phallic symbol. That cat was no ordinary cat. It was a pussy cat.

I recognized the girl behind the desk immediately, but covered it. There was amusement in her eyes, telling me she was in on the joke.

"Hello," she said. "How may I help you?" She made it sound as if it would be surprising indeed if I might actually have some legitimate business with the company. And her English had suddenly improved. She had a British accent that bespoke upper-class origins and the best preparatory schools. Chawlie, you old dog, I thought, bringing in an accomplished actress for the part. She was so good it was difficult to believe it was the same woman as the little China Girl whore who had visited my boat. But those were the same eyes, eyes a man could fall into and drown.

"Good morning. My name is Harold Jenkins from the Fidelity Casualty and Life Insurance Company of Seattle. Would Mr. Thompson be in, by any chance?" I handed her one of Jenkins's business cards, letting her see the others behind it.

"You don't have an appointment, do you?" she knew her lines and performed them flawlessly.

"No. Sorry I didn't call first. I need to speak with Mr. Thompson about his former tenant, Mary MacGruder. I don't mean to inconvenience Mr. Thompson in any way, but if I could speak with him it would help to clear up some final details. I'd like to close the file." I managed to include both a conspiratorial and a slightly suggestive tone to the last sentence.

"Please wait here, Mr. Jenkins," said Jasmine, the joy of the game unmistakable. She winked at me as she got up and pranced back to the inner office with the enthusiasm of a young colt. There was no trace of her other role. I suddenly worried for her. She was enjoying it too much. So much so that it showed. Chawlie would have to rein her in. People were dying. She was a little too headstrong to play this game with those kinds of risks.

"Mr. Thompson can see you right now but he asked me to tell you that it can only be for a few minutes. He is a very busy man." Jasmine was standing at the door, holding it slightly ajar.

It was not surprising Thompson would see me, if only for a few minutes. Anything even vaguely related to the death of

Mary MacGruder would be of interest to him. He either had some sentiments about the girl, or he had some involvement and would want to see if he could learn what other people knew about the investigation. The insurance con had been the perfect approach because it was both innocuous and believable. I hoped it wouldn't be wasted. There would not be another chance.

"Thank you," I said.

She stepped out of the way as I went through the door, giving me a wide berth.

Carter Allen Thompson stood behind a marble slab that served as a desk, allowing me to get the full sense of the man. He was big, and he was tall, a bodybuilder with a lot of free weights and chemical muscle development in his past. Dark, with an almost perfect machine tan. In his midthirties, he seemed bursting with health and power, yet there was little life in him. His eyes were small and dark, devoid of expression and just a little too close together for the broad brown face. I could read nothing in those eyes. He had a square jaw filled with square white teeth. Everything about him was blunt. I got the impression of a chunk of lava.

Dai-sho hung on the wall behind him, a matched pair of samurai swords that would be worth hundreds of thousands of dollars if they were authentic.

"Mr. Jenkins." Thompson's voice was surprisingly high and thin for a man his size, and unmistakably Australian. He extended his hand to me and I shook it, recognizing the calluses I felt as the hand of a serious *karate-ka,* evidence of thousands of hours of work at the craft. Combined with the weightlifting, I understood that I was in the presence of a man who worshiped at the altar of the body. On another level my mind began planning how I could make this work against him.

"As my secretary told you I only have a couple of minutes, but I want to do anything I can to help. Sit down, please." He pointed me toward an overstuffed leather chair in front of the desk, one of a pair.

I decided to abandon my pretense and go for the big lie.

"My name isn't Jenkins and I have nothing to do with insurance," I said, watching his response. When none came I continued. "My name is John Caine. I needed to see you and I thought that pretending to be an insurance agent would allow me access to you. It worked." I studied his expression as I was talking and was astounded to see absolutely no trace of a reaction. His expression could have been carved from stone.

"You have a young man named Garrick Choy working for you," I continued, launching into the carefully written script. "He's into a bookie and a loan shark and he can't get them off his back. He's trying to pay the loan shark by skimming off your take of an operation he's overseeing for you in Chinatown. The word is that he's been skimming for months, and he's into you for over a quarter million dollars so far. I know he's disappeared. And I know where to find him."

The bluntness of my statement, made without preamble, shook Thompson. He was not good enough to hide it when it finally hit home.

"What do you want?" He had taken the mental leap over the fact that I was not here to talk about Mary MacGruder.

"Parity. Check out what I told you about Choy. It's golden. Call me. Then we'll talk." I gave him a white business card containing only my name and cellular telephone number and got up to leave.

"Wait. How do you know about Choy?"

"Think of me kindly. You won't find him on the streets. Call me when you've audited your books."

I wasn't sure but I thought I saw him reaching for the telephone on his desk as I left his office.

Jasmine had one foot on her chair and was inspecting her toenails when I came through the reception room. For a second time in several days I was treated to the sight of lovely thighs. She smiled and winked at me. Harold Jenkins would have chastely averted his gaze, but John Caine looked her straight in the eye and winked back.

If what Chawlie and I suspected about Thompson was correct he would have people watching for me to exit the building. I made it easy for them and stopped at the bank on the first floor to exchange a couple of hundred-dollar bills for twenties and tens.

It was raining in the mountains above Honolulu and the sun was behind me. A broad rainbow straddled a peak, one of its feet planted in Punchbowl Crater at the end of Bishop Street. As I slowly wandered up Bishop admiring the rainbow I noticed two men twenty yards back, following me on foot. We had anticipated a car, too. If Thompson was serious there would be two cars.

I crossed the street and traveled the short block to the Fort Street Mall, a pedestrian thoroughfare. That eliminated the cars. As I crossed, I memorized every vehicle on the street. If I saw any of them again, I would file it as a possible. We didn't want a confrontation. Chawlie and I had agreed that would be counterproductive. We wanted to demonstrate to Thompson that he was not dealing with either the police or an amateur. And we didn't want anyone hurt in the process.

The two men shadowing me were haole bodybuilder types,

not first-string material any way you looked at them. I named them Tweedledum and Tweedledee; they vaguely reminded me of those two characters from *Alice in Wonderland*. They looked like bouncers from a tough club, gym rats taking on a day job.

When I was certain they were following me I reversed course and went down Fort Street toward the harbor, then ducked into Liberty House and paraded through women's wear and cosmetics and then back out onto Bishop again. Once outside I headed east toward the Iolani Palace.

Traffic was unusually light in a city that reluctantly admits to more automobiles per capita than any other place on earth. I noticed a red Maxima traveling slowly in the same direction but on the opposite side of the street. It had been behind me on Bishop when I crossed earlier. Two men were in it, both intent on my itinerary.

I cut across the grounds of the palace, taking the narrow footpath between the grounds of the state capitol and the barred iron fence of the royal palace. My Jeep was parked in the underground municipal garage one block away. Tweedledum and Tweedledee were doggedly following and now looked as though they were trying to decrease the distance between us.

We emerged from the footpath together and waited for the light to change. My shadowers had closed the gap to less than ten feet, letting me know they were there. We were almost at the underground garage and I sensed that their intentions were not merely watchful. They had a message to deliver. If they were just going to follow me they would have been more discreet. This was about to get physical.

I took off my jacket, feeling the solid impact of the Honolulu summer sun on my back through my thin shirt.

Just as the light changed I felt the two men closing in on either side of me. We stepped off the curb and crossed the street in unison. Naked aggression was out in the open but I continued to ignore the two men. I centered myself in anticipation of what was coming.

I attacked as we entered the gloom of the concrete ramp to the underground parking structure. They might be concerned with witnesses but that wasn't a concern of mine.

I dropped my aluminum briefcase. Both men looked down at the source of the noise. While Dee's head followed his gaze, I hit him in the temple with my right elbow, spun left and kicked Dum's shins as he reached for me. I followed the low kicks with kites delivered to his throat and face. He backed off, startled but not injured.

Dee had gone down. He started to get up. A roundhouse kick caught him on the point of the chin and he fell back, his head bouncing off the concrete. Dum recovered and grabbed for my arms. I reversed his grip, getting inside of his grasp, elbowed him in the chin, pounded his ears and raked my fingernails down the front of his face. He backed off again. I backpedaled and kicked him in the solar plexus.

Dum wasn't finished. Neither was Dee. They were merely angry. There was no room to maneuver in the narrow passage and they were crowding me. Dee grabbed my right arm and pulled me toward him. I went with it, using his momentum and the power to get inside his reach. I dropped my shoulder and smashed into him. We went down together. I shoulder-rolled over Dee and got to my feet as Dum charged, roaring in pain and anger.

I glanced behind to be certain I had room, and stood my ground.

As Dum charged, I caught his outstretched arms and rolled backward, one foot planted solidly in the middle of his chest. As my shoulders touched the concrete I brought the other foot up and launched him overhead. He sailed over me and I heard his heavy body hit the cement beyond. I completed my roll and stood up.

Dee was on his feet again, staggering toward me. I could hear Dum cursing behind, still down but working on getting up. I jumped over him and retreated to the expanse of the garage.

They followed. Dum was enraged, his bleeding face purple in the dim flourescent light. He had lost the bandanna that covered his head pirate fashion. His bald head was bleeding. An ear was torn where I'd noticed a gold earring before. Dee looked dazed but angry. This was going to get nasty unless I ended it now.

Dee was first. I kicked him in the leading shin, knocking his legs from under him. As he fell I reversed and kicked him in the temple. I whirled and attacked Dum, driving him back under a barrage of kicks and kites that would have killed a smaller human being. He absorbed the blows but didn't fight back. He couldn't fight, but I couldn't down him. I increased my attack, my arms and legs straining to sustain the rhythm. I was tired and I would be sore, but this thing had to end.

I backed Dum into the side of a parked van. He cowered, covering his head with his massive arms. I worked on his stomach muscles. They had been hard as stone when I first started hitting him. Now they were loose, a good sign. When he covered his middle I went to work on his face. Blood flew from my hands as I struck him. It was brutal. A referee would have stopped it and given me the decision. But this wasn't sport, there wasn't any referee and the only decision was for Dum to quit.

That's just what he did.

He put his hands out in front of him, palms forward. "Enough," he said.

He began to slump but I supported him, holding him upright until he could stand on his own.

"You okay?" I asked.

He shook his head. "Going to be sick." And he was.

I left him to his business and checked his partner. He was down, but he was conscious. I extended my hand to help him up. When he took it I helped him to his feet and then walked up the ramp and retrieved my jacket and briefcase. Both men were still there when I returned, as if moving was too painful to contemplate. They had no fight left.

"Give Mr. Thompson a message for me, will you?"

They nodded, pain and confusion written on their faces.

"I live at the Rainbow Marina in Pearl Harbor aboard the yacht *Duchess*. I gave him my telephone number and now he's got my address. After he finds out I was telling the truth, have him call me."

They nodded.

"You going to be all right?"

They nodded again.

"You boys are tough. Better go see a doctor, though, just to be sure."

I carried my briefcase to the Jeep and stuck it behind the seat. I folded my jacket. It would have to go to the cleaners. My shirt and pants were torn and bloody. They'd go into the trash. It was a small price to pay to learn what I had learned.

The consensus was correct. Thompson was not a nice man. He had people working for him who weren't very nice, but they weren't very good, either. If this was an object lesson directed at me it had backfired, leaving him in even greater ignorance than before.

The John Caine whom Thompson had seen was an enigma. He had come bringing gifts and then beat up Thompson's bouncers. He shook the tail Thompson had hung on him and then volunteered his address. None of it would make any sense.

If Katherine Alapai and Chawlie were right about Thompson it would keep him off balance and interested enough to want to keep me alive until I could find out if he had anything to do with Mary's murder.

I drove out of the garage and nearly collided with the red

Maxima. I stopped at the entrance and motioned to the driver to roll down his window.

"They're in there," I said, pointing back toward the garage. "Better call an ambulance."

I drove off, content with the confusion I saw on their faces.

VVVVVVVV

13

The next two days dragged as I waited for the bait to be snapped up by the big fish. Somewhere out there something was happening, but it sure wasn't happening where I could observe it. Chawlie agreed that Thompson was not the kind of man who could ignore the bait. It bothered me to know he was out there doing something, but not to know exactly what he was doing.

My body was sore from two fights in less than a week. That was a record, even for me. I limped. Somehow I'd acquired a deep bruise on the top of my shoulder. I was getting too old to be rolling around on the ground with men half my age.

For punishment of my sins I looked for hard physical labor. That isn't difficult to find aboard any boat. It's even easier aboard a wooden sailboat in the tropical Pacific. I discovered some railing that had become infested with dry rot. It was curved railing and had to be pieced. I spent some slave time and earnest money removing the damaged wood and replacing it with new solid teak. By the time I'd sanded the last section of railing smooth and oiled the new teak to match the old, the second day had nearly ended without contact from Thompson.

It was beginning to appear that Chawlie and I had erred in our assessment of the man.

I went for a run, showered and changed, and was sitting on my fantail watching the sunset, drinking a good merlot and thinking about a steak dinner, when my cellular telephone buzzed.

"Caine."

"Mr. Caine. My name is Anthony Choy. We met the other night. The man you know as Chawlie wishes to speak with you tonight, if possible. He says it is most urgent."

"Is he all right?"

"He would appreciate a visit from you at your earliest convenience."

"Please tell him I'll be there this evening."

"Thank you, Mr. Caine. I shall inform him."

I pushed the End button. A feeling of dread passed through me. Had we miscalculated? Chawlie was not calling for me because he wanted to celebrate. Mr. Choy was another of Chawlie's nephew-sons, possibly a brother or a half brother of Garrick Choy. Chawlie was sending me a message. In the convolutions of his thought processes this was probably a fairly straightforward proposition, but I was having trouble keeping up.

I finished the merlot and went below to put on my sandals. Chawlie would be there by the time I could drive to Chinatown. There was no reason to delay the inevitable.

Passing through the lounge I spotted the morning's *Advertiser*. Remembering a headline I hadn't explored earlier I picked it up and glanced through it again. On the third page of the first section I found the small article. A young Asian male had been found dead in a cane field near Waipahu. He had suffered a single gunshot wound to the back of the head, execution style. He had also suffered other, unspecified injuries. The story didn't say so but implied that the man had been tortured. Police suspected organized crime involvement. His identity was being withheld pending notification of the next of kin. End of story.

It was short, simple and succinct. I made a bet with myself the name of the young man was Garrick Choy.

Chawlie's eyes held no emotion when he saw me. He motioned for me to sit in a vacant chair next to him, not the chair across from him, my usual position. That one was occupied by the young Chinese man I'd known as Mr. Anthony Choy. Mr. Choy was dressed in a business suit with a bright red silk tie and handkerchief. Chawlie directed a string of harsh Cantonese at the young man.

"Good evening, Mr. Caine," said the young man. "Thank you for coming. I am Anthony Choy, the one who telephoned you. We have met before."

Chawlie barked a short sentence. He was not looking at me. I glanced at the side of his face. It could have been carved from ivory, as much expression as I saw there.

"I have been asked to speak for my father. He is in mourning for the loss of his son, Garrick Choy, but he wishes to convey to you both his gratitude and his sorrow for having used you the way he did."

Chawlie spoke another string of Cantonese. Anthony Choy replied quietly and respectfully. I watched young Choy's face during the exchange. He was fearful of something in the transaction, and he disapproved. There was no insubordination, but he was making it clear through his body language that his approval was not complete. I couldn't understand what was being said, but I followed the conversation. Chawlie was telling the young man to tell me everything, to leave nothing out.

"My father regrets that he is unable to speak with you directly. It is a form of mourning he has chosen that he wishes only to communicate with members of his family. He says he has a great sorrow because he has lost a son as well as a friend. He wants you to know that both losses are acceptable to him. Because he respects you he wants you to know this."

I kept silent and listened. I didn't like what I was hearing, but I wanted to hear it all.

"You know that my father had men keeping my brother safe and away from this problem for his own protection. Some time after you spoke with the Australian devil Thompson, my brother escaped from those who were watching him. The men guarding him didn't know he was gone until much later. By then it was too late.

"My father thinks he ran directly to Thompson, not knowing you had informed on him or that Thompson was hunting him. We don't know anything for sure. We only know that the police have been here and told my father that his youngest son is dead."

The old man leaned forward and said something in a voice so quiet I couldn't hear the words or even make out the language. The young Choy nodded, his eyes vacant.

"Father said it was fate that sent you to him the night he decided to do something about Garrick. He had asked for help and you suddenly appeared. You had been the solution to a previous problem and he saw you as the solution to his present dilemma. You were the solution to his problem as he was the solution to yours."

Chawlie spoke again. He spoke for a long time. Anthony Choy nodded and looked as if he were memorizing every word of what was being said to him. I had the impression it was not the first time he had heard it.

"Father wishes to convey three things to you. First, he is grateful for your service, both past and present, and he wants to justly compensate you." Choy pulled a thick sheaf of bills from his left coat pocket. "Father believes ten thousand dollars is adequate compensation.

"Second, Father wishes to assure you that he bears you no ill will for your part in the death of his son. It was fate. You were only the messenger and did not control the son who fled protection or the gun that killed him. Father understands that you are working for another father, one who lost a daughter, and if the loss of a son can help another father's loss, then it will not have been wasted. Father tells me that he understands the sorrow a father has for a lost child, even if that child is only a female.

"Third, I am to tell you that Father wishes never to see you again. For any reason. You shall always wear the mark of his dead son. Had it not been for you, Garrick might still be alive. Father will always be grateful to you for what you did for him, but he will have you killed if you try to approach him again.

"These are all the things Father wanted me to say to you. You have one minute to leave this place." He glanced down at his watch.

I looked at the old man beside me. Chawlie was staring out into the night, refusing to shift his gaze toward me. There was no appeal. He'd arranged it so everybody lost. I'd only lost a friend. He'd lost both a friend and a son. And his son had lost his life. All in the dubious name of family honor.

"Tell Mr. Choy I am sorry for his loss," I said. I got up and left the restaurant. There was nothing else to do.

Once outside again I took a deep breath, inhaling fragrances as familiar as my own sweat. I believed Chawlie's threat. I believed he would regret having me killed. But I knew he would do it as easily as he had arranged for the murder of his own son. I didn't believe for a minute that Garrick Choy had escaped on his own. It was the only solution the old man could find to save the family's honor. He had to let the young man escape and find his own way. If he died in the process, it was not Chawlie who had killed him. It was the Australian devil Thompson and that fool Caine.

My feet began walking away from the river without a conscious decision on my part. I clutched the sheaf of hundred-dollar bills in my hand. I didn't remember taking the money. I had no use for it. I walked east until I found the small cathedral on Fort Street. I thought a church, any church, was the best place for the blood money. I entered the church, not knowing what I was looking for.

An elderly priest sat in one of the pews, halfway down the center aisle, his head bowed. I didn't feel as if I belonged there. I stuffed the money into the poor box and went back out into the warm, tropical night.

Say a prayer for me, Father.

VVVVVVVV

14

The little red light on my answering machine was blinking when I returned home. I ignored it. I didn't want to talk to anyone until I secured *Duchess* for the night. Boats are like women. They require a lot of care. If they get it they will respond to you every time. Ignore them, and you'll lose them. I understand that's not politically correct. It's merely correct.

I pulled in her lines and secured her for the night. There was a little wind and chop, indications that Hawaii might be in for some heavy weather. We'd already had our hurricane for the decade, and even though we were in prime hurricane season I didn't think we'd get one. Iniki missed Honolulu at the last minute but savaged both the Waianae Coast of Oahu and the island of Kauai. The winds never rose above tropical storm levels in Pearl Harbor, and *Duchess* and I rode out Iniki in the middle of the harbor with the engine running and two anchors out.

When I was satisfied my boat wouldn't shift I went below and stared at the Stephen Hawking book. That lasted about five minutes because the words wouldn't come together. I was restless, dissatisfied with the way this thing was going. I was supposed to find the killer of one father's child. Another father had sacrificed his son for reasons I could not comprehend. I was the unwilling instrument of that sacrifice and I didn't like it.

Being used goes against everything I am. That's why I'm not employed by the big corporations or out working for a cause. There are no regulations on what I do. I submit no plans for approval. I have no review committee or inspectors to point out my errors. I labor under the illusion that I am free. When someone like Chawlie comes along and demonstrates that I am not as free as I'd like to think I am, the facing of that reality is threatening. We all like to have our illusions.

I made some coffee, the standard stuff, not the special roast. Tonight was not a night to celebrate. Tonight was not a night for another drink, either. I had not eaten dinner, but the thought of food made me queasy.

My cellular telephone rang.

"Caine."

"This is Thompson. Come to my office to see me. Tonight." The man's voice made my skin crawl, like listening to fingernails scratching a blackboard.

"Sorry."

"Excuse me?"

"Not tonight. Call me tomorrow."

"But you can't . . ."

I hung up.

The phone rang.

"Caine."

"I want you down here right now!"

I hung up.

The phone rang again. It may have been my impression, but the ring sounded angry.

"Caine."

"Mr. Caine." Thompson's voice betrayed his anger, but he was trying to retain control. "I told you to come down to my office for a reason. You obviously want something from me. You gave me information that turned out to be exactly correct. Now I wish to meet with you to discuss what you want in return. Tonight."

"Thompson," I said, "I don't take orders from anyone, so I don't take orders from you. If you'd like to see me, then ask, don't order. Taking orders can get to be a habit, and I have all the bad habits I need at the moment."

After a moment of silence he said, "Can you come down to my office?" The effort in his voice was tactile.

"What's the magic word?"

There was a pause.

"Are you serious?"

I didn't reply. I just waited.

"Please?"

"Sorry. Can't come down tonight," I said. "Call me tomorrow."

I hung up.

It was childish and vastly stupid. I may have blown my only lead, if that lead was to Thompson. I knew I was not only reacting to my revulsion to Thompson himself, but also to what Chawlie had done.

I thought Thompson might call in the morning anyway. My strange behavior could have had the opposite effect. My refusal might even increase his interest.

At least I hoped so.

The blinking light on my answering machine caught my attention again. I looked at the digital display. Someone had called while I was in Chinatown. I pushed the Play button.

"Mr. Caine, this is Detective Katherine Alapai, Honolulu Police Department. We want to interview you regarding the death of one Garrick Choy. I need to know how you were involved in this. Call me for an appointment. You have the number.

"Bring a lawyer, if you feel you need one."

15

"This is Katherine Alapai, homicide detective, Honolulu Police Department, interviewing John Caine." She stated the date and time and the fact that we were in her office at the main Honolulu police station. She had me repeat my name, age, address and occupation. This time I said I was a private detective, working for the family of a murder victim. It had a nice official ring to it. If this thing got nasty, I wanted everything on tape to sound official.

"Mr. Caine, are you aware that this conversation is being recorded?"

"I am."

"And you have consented to the recording of this conversation?"

"I have."

"And are you waiving counsel at this time?"

"I am."

Katherine looked at me, her black eyes penetrating my feigned nonchalance. I was reminded we were not playing games.

"Mr. Caine, can you tell me your relationship to the deceased?"

"Who?"

"Mr. Garrick Choy."

"I never met him."

"Never?"

"Not once that I'm aware."

"Are you aware that Mr. Choy worked for CAT Productions?"

I hesitated, reviewing my options. I decided that she would not have asked the question unless she already knew the answer.

"Yes," I said.

"And what is your relationship with CAT Productions, CAT Enterprises or Carter Allen Thompson?"

"I met Mr. Thompson three days ago in his office downtown. It was the first and only time we've met. My meeting with him lasted approximately three minutes. I have not seen him since."

Please don't ask the question, I thought.

"What did you discuss with Mr. Thompson during your meeting?"

Thank you.

"I am looking into the death of Mary MacGruder, a young lady who lived with Mr. Thompson. I thought he could help."

"Have you spoken with him since?"

Damn!

"Yes," I said. "Last night. He called me."

"What did he want?"

"He wanted me to come to his office. I refused."

"You refused?"

"Yes." I wouldn't give her any more than she asked for. I had too much respect for her intuition and abilities.

"Why?"

"I didn't want to." If she kept at it, her questioning would begin to resemble that of a precocious three-year-old.

"Care to elaborate?"

"No."

She angrily snapped off the recorder.

"God damn you, Caine!"

"What?"

"You're not telling me anything!"

"What do you want to know?"

"I want to know why that young man was murdered. You know! I know you know! And I know you had something to do with it!"

"Maybe I should call my lawyer," I said.

"Do you think you need one?"

"Now you stop it," I said. "You know I didn't kill that kid."

"I know you have the MacGruder file, and I know that you and I discussed Thompson four days ago, and I know that last night the kid was dead. He worked for Thompson. I know that three days ago you had a meeting with Thompson in his office, and immediately after that you got into a brawl with two of his men in the municipal garage. We followed you and watched you hurt those men. I know you've contacted Garrick Choy's father, both before and after he was murdered. You're into this up to your neck.

"That boy was tortured before he was killed. The medical examiner told me this afternoon that he had been kept alive for twenty-four hours before they killed him and when they did kill him he was better off. I want some answers and I want them now!"

"Unofficially I'll tell you everything you want to know. If you want me to talk into that recorder, or with a court reporter present, you'll get just what I'm giving you."

"Shit."

"Exactly."

"I can hold you as a suspect or a material witness."

I held out my hands in front of me, inviting the handcuffs. "I ought to take you up on that."

My hands remained where they were.

She glared at me. I didn't dare tell her at that moment, but when she is angry she is an incredibly beautiful woman. She drops her defenses and forgets to deny her beauty.

"Okay. Let's begin again." She reached for her notebook, leaving the recorder alone.

"Not here," I said.

"Kelly's again?"

"Kelly's again."

"Shit."

"Coffee," I said. "And if you're good, maybe some banana pancakes."

"You asshole."

"Just doing my job, Detective."

"You pay."

"That's fair."

We went in separate cars. She drove a midnight blue five-liter Mustang. The City and County of Honolulu pays its police officers to use their own vehicles. They can use them both for personal and official transportation. It's a cost-saving thing for the city, and it's good for the officers, too. There are certain cars they can't drive, such as the ones with puny little engines like mine. They are required to have eight cylinders under the hood.

She beat me to Kelly's and commandeered a booth in the back of the restaurant.

"I ordered you coffee," she said, smiling sweetly at me. I didn't know if it was a trap or if I had been forgiven.

"Okay," I said. "Here is the story." I told her about my meeting with Chawlie and how we had developed the scheme to wedge my way into Thompson's office. I related the short meeting with Thompson as well as I could. I didn't tell her about the source of the file, or that Chawlie's little actress was now playing spy in Thompson's production company. I told Katherine that at the time both Chawlie and I thought his son was protected, as Chawlie had him under house arrest. The subsequent meeting with Chawlie and the standing order for my execution should I ever approach him again was not mentioned, either. That was between Chawlie and me. I concluded with a recitation of my conversation with Thompson the night before, and about my hanging up on him.

"Did he call you again?"

"This morning. I have a meeting with him in an hour."

"Would you wear a wire?"

"Are you nuts?"

"Where are you going to meet?"

"I'll tell you after it's over."

"Mr. Caine . . ."

"Call me John."

"John. You've got to cooperate with me. I want this guy."

I nodded. "Me too, Detective."

"Call me Kate."

"Kate. I want to survive this thing. If I tell you, you'll put surveillance on me. If they drive a red Maxima they're not very good. And if they're not very good they could get me killed."

"Red Maxima, huh?"

I nodded.

"You noticed them?"

"Like they waved, and shouted, 'Yoo-hoo! Over here!'"

"Shit."

"That's what I thought of them, yes."

"I'll have them replaced. I didn't think you'd notice."

"Thanks."

"You're starting to surprise me, John. I followed up on Souza's suicide. It doesn't look like a suicide anymore. A detective went out and interviewed the landlady. We're reopening the case. You gave good information there."

"I got lucky," I said.

"Yes," said Kate. "You did. And you think this one's connected to Mary MacGruder and Garrick Choy?"

"Of course. Don't you?"

She nodded. "I know more about this case than I can tell

you. I wish I could, but it's impossible. If you're good and if you're still lucky you'll find out. If you do, we can compare notes. With confirmation of what I think I know we can nail him." Kate's eyes told me she wanted to tell me. "He's a very dangerous man."

"He's a stone killer," I said, thinking of Mary MacGruder and a boy in a cane field and the hot, musty apartment where the private investigator had been murdered.

"This meeting. What are you going to do? He must be curious about you."

"I won't know until I get there. It depends on him. I was vague about what I wanted. He wants to know that as well as the source of my information about Choy, and why I don't just fall down and worship him."

"He has a pretty high opinion of himself."

"Way too high," I agreed. "But I can help him with a lesson in humility."

"You'd do that."

"All part of the service."

"You'd better watch it," she said.

"I'll get by."

"That's not what I meant. You seem to suffer from the same handicap. Who's going to teach you humility?"

"You're doing a pretty good job," I said, and sipped my coffee.

VVVVVVVV

16

Despite what she knew about Thompson's nasty proclivities, Kate still arranged to have me followed when I left the restaurant. Even as she told me to be careful she was arranging for my escort. She had to know she'd put me in a precarious position if my tail was discovered, but catching Thompson was more important. It's always good for a guy to know where he stands.

At least they weren't the same people she'd hung on me before. This team was a couple, a man and a woman. They tried to look like tourists but they were so local and out of place it would be a hard sell if anyone was really looking. They drove a late-model silver Pontiac Grand Prix that looked like a rental, except rentals don't have the antenna array even the most obscure police cars are sporting these days.

Finding a tail isn't difficult. A retired FBI agent taught me the fundamentals one hot Saturday afternoon a few years ago. He called it a talent search. If you think you have someone behind you, turn right, then turn right again. Repeat that two more times and you are heading in your original direction. If there's anyone behind you after that, there's only one reason: they want to know where you are going.

I spotted my tail as soon as I'd completed half of my talent search. At the fourth turn I was certain it was a police tail. They were too discreet to work for Thompson. The couple's car was more powerful than mine and they had access to other police units if they lost me, possibly a helicopter. I knew I wasn't going to outrun them.

The light at Kapiolani and King changed from green to red. The intersection is near Honolulu Hale, city hall, about two miles from Waikiki. I stopped between a white rental car and a city bus. I set the parking brake and got out of the Jeep, leaving the engine running. I joined the throng of pedestrians crossing the street, moving with the crowd, walking along at its ambient speed.

I disappeared around the corner as horns began blaring.

Once out of sight I found a cab idling in front of a topless bar. I climbed into the back of the old Cadillac.

"Black Orchid."

"Sure t'ing," said the driver.

The Black Orchid is in Restaurant Row, a cluster of modern steel and glass buildings along Ala Moana Boulevard. The restaurants are popular with the locals, probably because they're reminiscent of New York or California. There isn't a palm frond or a tiki torch in the place, and tourists are few and far between. The locals find it exotic.

I paid the driver at the entrance to the underground garage and walked inside. I made my way through the afternoon crowd in the mall to the Black Orchid, on the far end of the row. I caught the eye of one of the parking attendants lounging against the wall. It was a little early for dinner and there wasn't much for him to do.

"Car, sir?"

"Can you call me a cab?" I handed him a five-dollar bill.

"Yes, sir," he said, and ran to the telephone.

Two minutes later a battered Chevrolet stopped at the valet stand. I got into the front seat.

"Honolulu Yacht Club," I told the driver.

VVVVVVVV

17

Five minutes later I was standing on the main deck of *Pele*, a seventy-nine-foot Grand Banks motor vessel. I thought the name ostentatious, but in keeping with Thompson's image and ego. Pele was the old Hawaiian goddess of fire and volcanoes, the mother of the Islands and therefore all life.

Even though I was five minutes early, Thompson was waiting for me. The crew cast off as soon as I came aboard and the deep-water yacht left the harbor, heading into a hot Hawaiian afternoon.

"I must say I like your style, Caine," said Thompson. He smiled at me, a drink in his hand. He was dressed all in black, a black silk shirt with those puffy sleeves you see on the covers of period paperback romances, and he was wearing tight black trousers. In place of the glossy high boots that should have completed the outfit, Thompson wore sandals.

"Oh, I was angry with you at first, I'll admit that. No one hangs up on me. No one. But I thought about it and decided you were right. No man such as yourself should take orders from anyone."

"You flatter me," I said.

"You intimidate me."

"I do?"

"Yes. You barge into my office using a false name and a fraudulent story, and you bamboozle my secretary—poor girl, she's not over it yet—and then you hand me some solid gold information without so much as a 'please' or 'thank you,' and then you just walk out of my office.

"You solved a problem I didn't even know I had. Two problems, actually. The solution to one problem led me to another problem I didn't know I had. And that brought still another. And all with solutions, now that I know what I'm facing. Is that too enigmatic for you?"

"Yes."

"Wonderful!" He laughed. "It made me curious about you. When I had you followed you lured my men into a trap and beat them nearly half to death. And then gave them your address! I like your style, Caine! I like the message you sent me."

"What message is that?"

"If I want to know anything about you all I have to do is ask. But it's dangerous to fuck with you. How am I doing?"

"Not bad," I admitted.

"One of the boys is still in the hospital, you know. Something's broken inside."

"Sorry."

"Don't be. All part of the game, you know. You won. They lost. It could have been you." He eyed me closely for a response and came up empty. "Life's like that. Winners and losers, winners and losers. It's nature's way of sorting it all out." His dark eyes settled on me. I felt uneasy under their bleak, obsidian gaze.

"So tell me, Mr. Caine. What is it you want from me? I can offer you the late Mr. Choy's position. The pay is ten thousand a week. I, ah, seem to have a current opening."

"No thank you."

"Then what?"

"I just wanted to talk. I thought a little gift was appropriate."

Thompson laughed, a bellow from way down below the belt line. "A gift? Yes. It was a gift!"

The yacht cleared the harbor entrance. I wondered where we were heading but I didn't ask. It would come in good time. I found my center and tried to appear relaxed. The sun was still high in the sky and Diamond Head loomed brown and green above the Waikiki skyline. Along the shore the classic pink jewel of the Royal Hawaiian stood apart from the bland high-rise hotels surrounding her.

Pele continued on an easterly course, matching the southern shore of the island.

"We can talk out here, Mr. Caine. Any topic you wish. Nothing leaves here unless I want it to leave. And nobody leaves here unless I want them to leave."

I smiled directly into the face of the threat. The bully treatment was beginning. First the carrot and then the stick. I remembered what my first objective had been with this man. I had to keep him interested so he would want to keep me alive. I had no illusion that he liked me or even thought I could be useful. He was trying to get inside my head, nothing more. Once he had what he wanted he would do away with me.

Or try to.

"I'll treat you the way I like to be treated," I told Thompson. "If I want to know something about you, I'll just ask." He said nothing, keeping me under his searchlight stare. "Tell me all about Mary MacGruder."

He didn't seem surprised.

"You really want to know about that little slut?"

"Yeah," I said. "I really want to know about that little slut."

"You work for her father?"

I nodded. I was going on blind faith and instinct. I had an idea that might work. It was the only thing I could see that had a chance to convince him I was harmless.

"Just like the other fella? That private eye? Hell, you know he killed himself?"

97

"I heard he had help."

This time surprise did flash across his features. Just for an instant his brow wrinkled and then it was smooth again.

"The admiral wanted to find out about my operation in the worst way. Anything. Anything at all. Souza was nosing around my people, trying to get in the back door. He found out a couple of things that might have been important. Before he gave his report to the admiral he tried selling it to me. Double-dipping, I think you Yanks call it. I couldn't trust a man who did that. Could you?"

The threat was there. Chilled sweat flowed down my back. He knew.

"In the end I had to do away with him. You've guessed it, as I see. He was becoming a nuisance. Winners and losers, just as I said. And he was a loser."

"Big-time."

"I'm disappointed in you, Caine. I checked you out. I thought we could do some business."

"We can."

"You work for MacGruder."

"He wants me to find out if there is any evidence in the investigation that could backfire on him. Anything like drugs, or a hint of Mary's involvement in any kind of illegal activities. Things like that could ruin his career. I agreed to help, hoping to find the pot of gold. I think I could bleed him dry without a comeback."

Thompson laughed. "You're a sharpshooter!"

"Of course. Aren't you?"

He smiled. "Is that what you want? Is that all?"

"I need proof. Evidence. Something concrete I can show the admiral."

Thompson put down his drink. *Pele* had rounded Diamond Head and was headed along the rough coastline beyond. From Diamond Head to Sandy Beach it's all a rocky lava coast with little protective barrier reef. It's no place for boats to get into trouble. It's not a place where I wanted to swim to shore, either.

"You want evidence? How about a videotape? Come on." He went below, his broad back and shoulders nearly larger than the passageway and the hatch.

I followed him to the main cabin. There was a large-screen television in one corner of the salon. Jasmine was there, too, dressed in a black string bikini and matching high heels. Even though she was dressed for a party she didn't look the part. Her eyes were large and dark and red from crying. Bruises adorned her arms and legs. I recognized the signs of an expert beating, one that produced maximum pain.

"Jasmine, get out!" Thompson's hand became a fist. The girl scrambled out of the room, tripping once. He didn't raise his arm. He didn't have to. She went forward, the hatch slamming behind her.

"She made a mistake the other day, letting you in without first checking on you. You could have been a cop. I disciplined her. Had to. Ordinarily she likes to use my equipment but she doesn't like to hurt. She likes to pretend. She's quite the actress, you know." His eyes, knowing, gleamed in the low light of the interior of the vessel. "This time was a surprise for her. Instead of pleasure, she found real pain." Thompson watched me for a reaction. I gave him nothing.

He pulled a videotape cartridge from a nearby bookshelf and inserted it into the machine atop the television. "Sit," he commanded. "This won't take long, but it will be educational. You wanted evidence."

The tape lasted thirty minutes. I was reminded of someone, I don't remember who, who said that the first ten minutes of a pornographic movie made her feel sexy and the remainder made her want to give up sex forever. This one revolted me from the start. I found none of it arousing. I'll admit to being particularly offended because I'd become proprietary toward one of the participants. The fact that she was dead, and possibly by the hand of the man sitting next to me, didn't help.

All of the action took place in one room. The camera angle was stationary, never wavering during the entire film. There were no close-ups, no change of background, no overheads. It all took place in a single perspective. I memorized that background, looking for landmarks I could identify if I ever saw this room, or a photograph of the room again. The only visible wall was covered with teak paneling, and sand-colored carpeting covered the floor. There were no windows, which made me wonder if the film had been shot in a basement.

There was no plot. A nude Mary MacGruder was in it, but the star was a young girl who looked to be in her late teens. She appeared only mildly worried at first. I got the impression she wanted to believe she was only acting, but failed to convince herself. When the real pain came, enthusiastically administered by Mary, she screamed into the high registers. The girl was tied to a rack that exactly matched the sketch in the coroner's report. She was a blonde, too. A natural blonde.

It made the hair on the back of my neck stand up when I realized I was watching Mary MacGruder practicing her own demise.

I have never understood how people can take pleasure from other people's pain. It didn't make sense to me to take the most tender and loving of human acts and twist it like that. On the other hand I've lived long enough to know there are no depths to which the human soul cannot reach.

"It was a commercial enterprise," said Thompson. "All Mary's idea. I'd been doing skin flicks using blondes for years. The Japs love the stuff, can't get enough of it. They're so fucking macho this stuff really turns them on. And for them a blonde is a true exotic." He laughed. "They think they go this way." His finger traced a line horizontally.

"Mary put a spin on it. She hit on the idea of the bondage. She was into S and M anyway. I don't know where she got it, but believe me she was expert. She said the Japanese really liked it. I didn't know where she learned that tidbit, either, but I went along with her. She was quite the little salesperson.

"She recruited the girls. She built the rack. She insisted on acting in the movies. I paid for everything, took the videos and gave the girls the plane fare home. Sometimes I had to pay a doctor. It was rare, but it happened. Don't look so shocked. Professional football teams have a team physician, too, you know, and that's just for entertainment. I was the producer, just the producer, but Mary was the heart and soul of the enterprise.

"And Mary knew just how far to go. Most of the time. Sometimes she'd get a little too enthusiastic and my costs would go up for the settlements, but she loved it. She loved every part of it. And the extra money was returned many times over, because those special videos brought in much more money. The Oriental likes pain, you know, Caine, as long as it's not his. And if it's real, it's worth more money.

"What you just saw brings in five thousand a copy. And that's just the tame stuff. It's like stealing, only more fun."

"Are all of them like that?"

Thompson averted his gaze, his eyes hooded. "Most of them," he said.

"What about the rest?"

"Special tastes. They're only for a select clientele."

"Got any aboard?"

He looked past me, peering into something I could not see. The movie had aroused him, and he was annoyed by my presence and my questions. Mary MacGruder was not the only one who loved it.

"Maybe," he said. He shuddered, and brought himself into the present. "Can you keep your mouth shut? This isn't something I'm going to give away."

I nodded. I knew what I was into now. It was worse than I had imagined.

VVVVVVV

18

W hat do you have? Snuff films?" It took an effort to keep the horror from my voice, barely managing to keep it casual.

The burned-out coals Thompson used for eyes regarded me for a full ten count before he replied.

"That's going to cost you," he said. "Parity is what you said you wanted. If that's what you want we'll have to be partners. What can you bring to the party?"

"I don't know the extent of your operation—"

"Oh come on, Mr. Caine. I know your background. I checked you out. Give me a little credit."

"Access to MacGruder," I said.

"I should say so." Thompson smiled, his capped teeth looking like rows of little white tombstones. "For starters, you've got an admiral in the United States Navy who has trusted you with a valuable secret. Granted it's personal, but it's still valuable. Have you checked his resources?"

"There's money." I was skating along the edge of control, saying the first thing that came into my mind to stay in the game.

"That's all you know?"

I shook my head, unsure where this was going.

"No?" he asked in mock surprise. "Well, I have checked him out. I don't suppose you know that he is from the Virginia Mac-Gruders?"

I shook my head.

"You've heard about the Virginia MacGruders?"

"I'm ignorant of the subject."

"The *Mayflower* ring a bell?"

I nodded.

"The first MacGruder who counted in America was one Charles Winston MacGruder, a Scotsman, who just happened to be one of the officers of that fine vessel. His descendants remained. Since your Revolution there has been a MacGruder in the service of the United States Navy at either flag rank or as a lowly captain. There's a family home in Virginia. It's been in the clan since the end of your Civil War, a reward, you might say, for services rendered to the Union.

"Two thousand acres. There have been three United States senators from Virginia with the MacGruder name. The last one was the current admiral's father.

"Your friend MacGruder is a member in good standing of the closest thing America has to a landed aristocracy. Back in feudal times, Admiral MacGruder would have been a nobleman, raising his own army or navy for the battle. Can you imagine how much cash a man like that can lay his hands on? Two thousand acres of prime real estate? He's got to be worth hundreds of millions of American dollars."

I thought about it and could not picture it. But then, that kind of money had never been a driving force in my life.

"You will note the absence of sons in the current family, the absence of any heir at all? The admiral's wife and daughter died within six months of one another, leaving him alone in his advanced years. He appears to be the end of the line."

"Which means . . . ?"

"Unlimited ability to pick his pockets."

"With access—"

"Absolutely."

"A snuff film with Mary's brand," I mused. "If MacGruder knows she played a part, and that we have the proof, he'll pay anything to protect his career and to protect his daughter's reputation."

"You've got that in the proper order, Mr. Caine. His career will always come first."

"What did he say when you approached him?"

Thompson looked at me sharply. For the second time today I'd taken him by surprise.

"Did he tell you about that?"

"Yes," I lied. I'd made a guess and it appeared to have been a good one. I was getting information that wouldn't have been available otherwise. If only I knew where all this was going.

"Then you must be very close to the admiral. Or you caught him off guard."

"He saved my life a long time ago."

Thompson grinned, neat little capped teeth on display, so uniform they looked nearly pointed, his otherwise handsome features a Halloween mask. "He saved you so we could pluck him. That's wonderful."

"You have the tapes on board?"

Thompson nodded. He left the lounge and returned with a VHS tape cassette with a commercial label. The label featured a cartoon of Rex Harrison as Henry Higgins pulling the strings of a puppet I recognized as the actress who played Eliza Doolittle. I couldn't remember her name.

"My Fair Lady?"

"You like that?"

I wasn't interested in whimsy, but I smiled politely. He started the tape and fast-forwarded the machine, causing the opening dance numbers to fly across the screen. In the middle of a song-and-dance number there was a sudden overlay. The washed-out colors of the old production gave way to a muted but clear video picture of the same room in which Mary had previously participated. The camera angle was identical. The background was the same. Thompson slowed the tape to normal speed and the Hollywood production was replaced by the still life of the rack and the room, giving me a slight case of vertigo.

This time I noticed plastic tarps covering the carpet. I braced myself to watch what I did not want to watch, knowing what I was going to see.

At first the set was empty. The rack was featured in the foreground, the camera angle head-on. No imagination would be required. When the action began, two men led a docile and naked young woman into the camera's vision. There was no sound but the hiss and pops of the speakers, and I thought it was a silent video until one of the men coughed. The production was off to a slow start. The actors didn't appear to be certain what they were going to do. It occurred to me this might have been a first attempt.

The girl was frightened. I could tell she was in some kind of chemical cloud, but it wasn't deep enough to overcome her apprehension. The drug-induced placidity and the nervous tension combined to make her look like a slightly disturbed cow. Her face was plain and doughy in a way that reminded me of a younger version of the woman in *American Gothic*. She wasn't pretty in the classic sense, but youth flatters even the plainest of features. Her body, however, was spectacular, the classic Venus figure. In a few years, and after a couple of children, it would become a disappointment, but the camera caught her in full bloom, before time's assault started wearing down the tissues. Her breasts were perfect, full and round, with pink nipples pointed toward the heavens. She'd never had children. Her hips flared from a narrow waist. Strong, athletic legs supported her, or would have had she been able to stand on her own. The drug and her fear weakened her.

Mary MacGruder was not present. Two Asian males wearing nothing but black ski masks handled the girl, strapping her onto the rack. Both were physiologically affected by their task. I made a clinical appraisal of their bodies. They were not American bodies. Flabby and hairless, they had the typical Asian middle-management, middle-aged flaccidity that comes from spending years behind a desk with little or no exercise. These were merchants, predators of the marketplace, out for adventure.

I remembered a recent scandal in California where a rancher sold hunting rights on his land to deep-pocket businessmen. The "hunters" paid big dollars to shoot big-game animals on the ranch. All of the animals were either tied to posts or in cages when the "hunters" shot them. It made me wonder what these assholes paid for the privilege of raping and killing this helpless girl.

Her mouth was gagged with a rubber ball, kept in place with an elastic tube around her head. I'd never seen anything like it, but it effectively cut off any attempt at screaming. The camera never moved during the preparations, and no words were exchanged between the two men. It was a sweaty, tedious demonstration of inefficiency. The men's hands were shaking. Curiously, the girl attempted no protest, cooperating with her captors. That for me was the most disturbing thing of all.

I memorized the girl's face and body. I noted a small red tattoo on her right hip. It appeared to be a tiny red heart. I couldn't make out the caption that floated on her flesh above it. She had a keloid scar on her right knee, evidence of old ligament surgery.

And the resemblance of her face to the woman in *American Gothic* was striking. I knew I would never again be able to look at that painting without remembering this girl.

After some preliminary preparation, one of the Asians mounted the girl and grunted against her. It reminded me of pigs mating, except pigs had more intelligence and gentility. He finished quickly, a little too quickly to suit the other man's taste. When he withdrew, his penis slack, his partner laughed and said something I did not understand. I listened intently. The language was Japanese. It was too fast for me, but I caught the word *sakanaya*, "fish market." The first man shook his head and replied, also in Japanese.

I looked to Thompson for clarification, but he wasn't listening. He was lost in the movie.

The second Japanese raped her. He was harsher and took longer. As his excitement built, he became rougher still, slapping the girl. The more excited he became, the harder he slapped her. The first man positioned himself behind the rack and slipped a piece of narrow white line around her neck.

I tried not to watch the screen but I made the mistake of looking at the girl's eyes. They were the only part of her body she could move. The second man neared climax and shouted to the first man. I didn't know what he said but his meaning was clear. The rope began to tighten. I watched the girl's eyes widen, pleading for help.

The man did a bad job of strangling her. It took a long time, but I could not take my eyes from her face. Finally her eyes lost focus. Even with the poor quality of the tape I could see the exact moment when her body went slack.

The man climaxed as life left her body.

He pulled himself out of her and helped his partner cut down the body. The way the corpse dropped to the floor it was obvious the girl was dead. I'd seen enough bodies to recognize the real thing. The rope was embedded in her neck as it had been in Mary MacGruder's.

This was how Mary died? As a play toy for visiting businessmen? Somewhere there would be a tape of the act. I had to get my hands on it and destroy it. It was something I could never show to MacGruder. And I didn't want anyone else to view it for pleasure or for justice. I wanted to bury the tape as deep as I could.

All the tapes.

I wanted to get my hands on Thompson and strangle him

as this girl had been strangled. But not yet. His time would come. I had a job to do first.

The picture faded and was replaced by Eliza Doolittle singing and gliding around what looked like a two-story English library set, an obscene counterpoint.

Thompson got up and rewound the tape. "If you run it backward you can bring her back to life," he said.

I didn't even smile.

"How much do you get for one of those?" I asked, distrusting my voice.

"Fifty thousand. In cash. The buyer can participate if he wishes, of course. He can take his pick: a blonde, a brunette, a boy, a girl, twins, whatever his tastes. Some requests are more difficult to fill and therefore more expensive. This is a small island and if we have to import for any reason the cost goes up. Disposal was a problem, too, but we managed to solve that."

"How many tapes do you have?"

"Trade secret, my friend. I can't tell you. But I can tell you that I will soon have enough to retire. And that is what I plan to do. Mary hit on a gold mine. Smart girl. Japan and Taiwan have an almost inexhaustible market, but I've got to be careful. I only sell by word of mouth. I have a very select clientele, as you can well imagine, and I'll only speak to a new customer upon the recommendation of a trusted and valued old friend."

"Mary think of this?"

"No. She was against the snuff, but she liked all the rest. She defied me, tried to set some girls loose I had collected for special orders from Japan.

"When she thought it was all for fun, when it was just fuck-for-money movies, she procured for me. You'd be surprised how many little tourist girls are willing to take their clothes off for five hundred dollars or free dope, especially if there's a beautiful young girl doing the selling. They felt safe. When it got rough, Mary didn't care. We'd calm them down afterward and convince them it was all fun and games.

"But Mary didn't like the idea of killing the girls. I think she had a soft spot somewhere inside of her, although I hadn't seen that before.

"It got so she threatened to take me to the authorities. She actually got away from me once and tried to hide out in the cane fields. Nearly succeeded, but my people found her and brought her back. Then I got tired of arguing with her and arranged for her own film. That one has a price of a hundred thousand. She was a trophy, natural blonde, admiral's daughter, and all that. And she was one beautiful woman. A lot of spunk. Had to give her a sedative to get her to cooperate, and then wait until it wore off before we could do the movie. She fought me all the way. It was wonderful. Would you like to see it?"

He smiled at me. I wanted to take a lamp and smash him with it repeatedly.

"No."

"Get kind of a queasy stomach? These aren't for everybody. But they make money."

"So where do we go from here?"

"Well, Mr. Caine, I'm going back to the yacht club for dinner. You're not going so far. As I said, we do special requests. We've just had one about man-eating sharks."

I glanced briefly out the porthole over his shoulder, at the rolling blue ocean beyond the railing.

"They're out there, you know. Big ones. Tiger sharks, whites, hammerheads. Man-eaters. And they get hungry right about now. You'll notice that it's three-thirty?"

I kept my gaze on Thompson. "I'll take your word for it."

"While we were watching the movie my men were chumming. Did you know that a shark can sense one part of blood in thirty million parts of seawater? We've been dumping gallons of blood into the ocean behind us for the past half-hour. By now I'm sure we've got some interested company.

"I'll miss my little secretary. She was a honey, but there's always another around. Pretty girls are completely replaceable." He clapped his hands. "Frank! Bring her now!"

I disagreed with him and said so. Pretty girls were a vanishing resource and should be protected and cherished whenever and wherever possible. They're like the trees in a rain forest. No matter how many there are, there are never enough.

"You put on a good act, Caine, but I know you're tight with Chawlie Choy, not MacGruder. His little actress told us all about your plan. She didn't want to, but . . . well, yes she did. In the end she wanted to tell us everything. It was very important to her to keep us happy."

I gripped the edges of the lounge chair. I'd brought a couple of weapons with me in case the party got rough. They were in inconvenient places but they were still there.

"Once you're out of the way MacGruder will pay up and Choy will leave me alone. This will be an object lesson for Choy. Losing three of his people in one week."

"Winners and losers," I said.

"Exactly," said Thompson, smiling his tombstone smile. "And I'm always the winner."

Tweedledee, one of the two shadows I'd met before, brought Jasmine into the lounge. She had not changed but she'd lost her high heels and gained a pair of handcuffs. Without her shoes she looked even tinier, like a lost child. The black bikini was in place, but loose, as though it had been dragged onto her by someone else. Her face was white. She knew what was happening and there was nothing anyone could do about it.

"Have fun in there?" Thompson treated the man he called Frank like a pet. After getting what he needed from Chawlie's spy he'd thrown her to him the way he would throw a bone to a junkyard dog.

Tweedledee smirked at me. He wore only purple Speedos. There were bruises on his face and arms and he moved carefully, as if any movement hurt. Acne raged across his back, evidence of long-term abuse of anabolic steroids. "We had some fun." He wrapped one palm around one of Jasmine's breasts, proclaiming ownership. His thumb and forefinger rolled a nipple back and forth beneath the spandex. She flinched, but said nothing. Her fear was absolute and all thought of resistance had fled.

I was dressed for yachting in a pair of loose khaki trousers, deck shoes without socks and a white polo shirt. I wore no watch and carried no wallet or identification, only a couple of bills in my right front pocket. I didn't even have the keys to my boat. They were still in the ignition of the Jeep. I did have some surprises. My belt buckle was a two-inch dagger, and a Phrobis knife was strapped upside down to my left calf. My fallback weapon was secured to the inside thigh of my other leg, snugged up tight against my groin.

Time was running out. I only hesitated because I wanted to see where the other two crew members had gone before committing myself. I heard a noise behind me and started to look around when somebody hit me on the back of the head.

I was surprised how much it hurt.

Then nothing hurt.

VVVVVVVV

19

When the world swam back into focus I found my hands cuffed behind my back. I was facedown on the deck, missing my shoes and shirt. The hot sun beat down on my bare back. Blood dripped from behind my left ear, puddling on the teak deck near my nose, smearing into my face and hair. The Phrobis knife was gone from its sheath, but my belt buckle still pressed against my stomach. I carefully rubbed my thighs together. The UM-1 bangstick, a small telescoping cylinder taped to the inside of my upper thigh, had not been discovered. And I was alive. That was the good news. I was handcuffed on a boat owned by a man who killed people the way McDonald's sold hamburgers. That was the bad news. That, and the heavy weight belt strapped around my waist.

A few feet away the two flimsy pieces of Jasmine's black bikini lay on the deck. A trail of quarter-size blood drops led to the railing.

A hand grabbed a fistful of hair and pulled my head from the deck.

"You thought you were clever, Caine." Thompson's voice was next to my ear, somewhere behind me. "It took only twenty-four hours to find what you were about. Giving me Choy's son was a wasted effort. It's true I didn't know about the theft, and I will use it against his father. And it helped me find his little spy. The old man owes me a big one for trying to infiltrate my organization.

"You and Choy killed that boy just to give you credibility. I can't say I don't admire that kind of cold-blooded thinking, but it didn't work. By the time the boy died I knew more about his old man than Choy will ever know about me. You did intrigue me, though. We needed to have this little chat. I'm still a little disappointed to find you were so easy."

"Don't let it get around," I said. "Ruins my reputation."

He slammed my face against the teak.

"I always appreciate style, Caine. Don't lose it."

While my head was raised I got a glimpse of where we were. It wasn't encouraging. *Pele* was about five miles off Makapu'u Point. These weren't good waters for swimming. There's a strong current running south and east, toward the island of Molokai, called the Molokai Express. It might be easier swimming the distance to that island than trying to get back to shore on Oahu. If the sharks didn't find me first.

"Mr. Caine, I'd like to continue our chat but you've got to go. The girl has already left us. There's a big brute out there, looks to be about a twenty-footer, reminded me of a small submarine. But it's a real tiger. Biggest shark I've ever seen. There's a smaller one, too, fifteen or sixteen feet. I don't think it got a chance to feed earlier, so it might be hungry.

"The big one made short work of the girl. Two bites. It was a short tape, too. Might disappoint the customer. But you're dessert."

And with that, strong arms lifted me from the deck and threw me overboard.

I hit the clear blue water with a tremendous splash. It sounded like a small whale breaching. That's one way to call sharks.

Sharks were not my first worry. I was sinking fast. Pressure on my ears was intense and increasing. I did what I could to clear them by yawning. That's hard to do with your mouth closed but the pain and disorientation of broken eardrums in addition to my other troubles right then would finish me.

I worked my cuffed hands down over my buttocks and thighs and finally to the back of my calves. The chain on the cuffs caught on the empty knife sheath. Ignoring a rising panic, I concentrated on the task at hand, determined to get it right, moving the metal links back and forth to try and free them. The chain suddenly came free and my hands were in front of me, the effort nearly dislocating my shoulders. I tripped the quick release buckle on the weight belt. One of the blocks of lead painfully rapped my foot as the heavy belt plummeted toward the depths.

I estimated I was over eighty feet down. The surface wasn't visible. Even in the clear water it was only a murky light above. Needing air, I stroked toward my own element.

My head found precious air fifty yards from the stern of *Pele*. It had taken every bit of willpower I possessed to keep my mouth closed and the pumps shut down. It felt so good to breathe again I nearly hyperventilated, bobbing around on the surface, enjoying the pleasure of oxygen.

Once my breathing returned to normal I checked my options. Now I could worry about sharks.

Pele's engines were idling. I kept my head as far down in the water as I could and observed the yacht. Thompson's men were searching the water, using binoculars. They were looking for me as if they'd expected me to defeat the weight belt and handcuffs. They were taking few chances.

Remembering Thompson's description of the two sharks, I unzipped my pants and pulled them down to my knees. The bangstick was securely taped to my thigh and it took some work to get it loose. I was floating in the warm Pacific like a tourist at Waikiki, traveling at a rate of two to three knots away from my island, but I had to get to the one piece of survival gear that might save me if those monsters returned.

I didn't know what to expect when I accepted Thompson's invitation for a cruise, but I don't make a habit of going to potentially unfriendly environments without a friend or two. Knowing Thompson's proclivity for using people until they weren't useful anymore I came to the party with more than just my smile. The knives were for whatever happened; they are the most useful weapons that exist. I'd rather carry a knife than a firearm even though I'm proficient with both. The UM-1 bangstick is an underwater defensive weapon and is issued to SEALs when they operate in shark-infested waters. Mine held a maximum-loaded .44 magnum cartridge with a soft-nosed jacketed slug. The bangstick would kill anything in the water up to fifteen or sixteen feet. It had an inertial trigger, so firing it meant striking the target. I hoped Thompson's report of a twenty-footer was an exaggeration.

I released the UM-1 from the tape on my thigh and snapped the two pieces into place. It was twenty-six inches long assembled, just long enough to keep the brutes away. It had three rounds, including the one in the chamber.

I pulled my pants up and secured the belt again with its vicious buckle. The little knife was my ultimate backup and I hoped I wouldn't need it.

With *Pele*'s crew still looking for me I started swimming toward Oahu. I'm a strong swimmer, but not Superman. Having my hands locked together was a handicap but now that my hands were no longer behind me, many things were possible. I knew fighting the current would be fatal so I swam at an angle to the drift, directly toward Waikiki. Once I got in the lee of the island I'd be out of the strong current and could head toward the beach. Diamond Head looked to be at least ten miles away. I wouldn't have to swim that far. Only six or seven. If nothing ate me I would make it by midnight.

I swam the combat swim I'd learned at Little Creek, Virginia, moving silently through the sea while making no waves or ripples. The technique didn't call attention to my presence and could be accomplished even with my hands cuffed together. *Pele* was still around. And then there were the other predators.

I wasn't afraid a shark would bite me before he investigated. Most sharks will circle and inspect a potential meal before taking action. I've been circled countless times. At that point an aggressive attitude will usually warn them off. Before they bite they like to bump the potential meal with their nose. They have skin like sandpaper, with little "teeth" covering their entire body. Run your hand down a shark's back and you're likely to shred your palm. When they bump a potential dinner they'll lacerate whatever they're interested in. If it bleeds, they'll sense the blood and then come back and dine.

Sharks are not brave creatures. They are also not smart. The little microprocessor they have for a brain has a "food" program. If you fit into the pattern you become food. If you don't, you don't. Most of the time. I fit two of the profiles as I understood them: I was swimming on the surface late in the afternoon. Sharks are nocturnal predators. They begin feeding about this time. And surface swimmers are one of their favorite meals.

But sharks are not machines. They usually circle, though not always. Hammerheads are notorious for going right for whatever they want, leading by their teeth. Last year a big tiger shark came into five feet of water and carried off a boy playing next to his mother on the shore. There was no preamble, it just struck without warning. I was concerned about that kind of shark wandering around in these waters. If I met one I'd have no chance at all.

I like to be at the top of the food chain. Out here in the pelagic currents, the top position can always be argued.

Something zipped by me, skipping off the surface of the ocean about a foot from my head. I recognized the authoritative bark of a high-powered rifle and submerged before a second bullet found me.

I swam straight down, jogged right and came up about thirty feet from where I'd submerged. The afternoon trades were beginning to pick up, blowing against the current. That meant the ocean would get rougher and I would have some swells to hide in. It also meant Thompson's platform would not be a stable one. I had to admire his concentration. Coming that close to a moving target on an open ocean was impressive marksmanship.

I dove to twenty feet. The clear water gave me more visibility than on the choppy surface. I could see about a hundred feet in all directions. I remained underwater as long as I could, surfaced and replenished my air supply, and then dove again. This time the hull of *Pele* came into view, about sixty feet away. I waited a little longer, hoping they would not see me as they searched the ocean. I remained underwater until my head felt as if it were filled with helium.

When I surfaced they were moving away from me at high speed, heading back toward Waikiki. I began swimming toward the black lava rock I called home.

I heard the engines coming back fast. Another shot hit the face of a wave five feet away, chunking into the water. Thompson was up on the bridge, shooting from a higher angle.

I went under again. More shots were fired down into the water around me. The boat stopped, reversing its props, hovering overhead. I moved under the shadow of the hull, mindful of the propellers. I needed air. The only place I could surface was near the bow where the overhang of the forward hull blocked the view from the deck.

I popped up, filled my lungs and dove again in one fluid motion, diving deep, angling under the hull. Tweedledee anticipated me. He was leaning over the forward deck when I came up. He fired a burst from an automatic rifle toward the place where I had been. *Pele* took off. Had I remained on the surface I would have been shot and then dragged into the propellers.

The Grand Banks moved about ten yards and slowly glided to a stop. I surfaced and dove again before I could take a breath, driven under by an intense barrage of automatic rifle fire. I couldn't go deep enough fast enough. A bullet hit me in the back of my leg, embedding itself in the soft flesh below my right buttock. The water had reduced the velocity of the bullet but it still penetrated and it still hurt. And it would bleed.

I surfaced, gulping air, ignoring the incoming rounds zinging overhead. The swells made it impossible to get a bearing on me, but spraying automatic fire was one way to get lucky. I dove again.

I'd had enough. I snapped both safeties off the UM-1 and swam toward *Pele*. When I was directly under the yacht I picked my spot and slammed the bangstick against the fiberglass. The inertial trigger fired, blowing a fist-sized hole in the hull. I dove deep, reloading as I swam.

Pele's propellers revved. The Grand Banks shuddered as the hull picked up speed and began to plane. They were quitting the fight.

I came to the surface. I couldn't find the yacht. Her engines were retreating, heading for less dangerous waters. If my calculations were correct, the bullet struck home in the lounge, somewhere in the vicinity of the television. If I got lucky, I hit the big-screen television. If I hit the jackpot, the bullet hit Thompson. Between the legs.

Pele's pumps would be strong enough to handle the water in the bilge, but the hole was a hell of an inconvenience and it would have to be repaired immediately. That meant the tape collection would be moved from the boat. Thompson couldn't afford to have workmen stumbling onto his collection.

All I had to do now was get ashore.

Yeah, right. Ten miles away the volcanic cones of Diamond Head and Koko Head stood like black sentinels against a pale sky. The sun was heading toward its rendezvous with the sea in the northwest, a trip that would take two to three hours. I wished I were at Jameson's in Haleiwa, sitting with friends and waiting for the sunset from their lanai bar.

I felt the bullet wound. Always the same leg. It wasn't a bad wound and it was bleeding freely so it wouldn't tighten up on me and it shouldn't get infected. It throbbed and that's as bad as it was going to get. It wasn't bad enough to kill me unless it attracted some curious, hungry, toothed visitors.

I wondered what Max would say. Shot again in the same damned leg. I hoped I'd get the chance to find out.

The sharks that took the girl had vanished as soon as I hit the water. All the commotion and the engine noise may have scared them off. But they'd be back. There was no question in my mind they'd be back.

It would be dark before I made it to shore. I was alone, bleeding and exhausted. My hands were cuffed. Even the most desperate life insurance salesman would not solicit me now. I was just what sharks like the best: a wounded, weak swimmer, far from home, leaking blood and splashing around on the surface. If I didn't ring their dinner bell, nothing would.

All I could do was swim toward Oahu and hope for the best. There wasn't another choice. Giving up was not a part of my repertoire. I was not in the best place, but I still had two rounds left in my bangstick, and if they were going to come for me I'd take as many of the beasts as I could before I became shark dinner.

All things considered, though, I preferred the company of the monsters in the ocean to the real ones aboard *Pele*.

VYYYYYY

20

I made steady progress for over two hours before the first predator came to investigate. There was still enough light in the sky to navigate and I saw the dorsal fin about twenty yards off, running parallel to my course. It was a big one. From the size of the fin I estimated it at close to fifteen feet. I ducked my head underwater and watched its approach.

It was a tiger, a big female. She sported scratches along her flanks, evidence of a recent mating.

I readied my weapon, making certain both safeties were off. The shark continued her circumspect approach. She was now ten feet away and edging closer. I could see the eye the size of a hen's egg watching me. It was a predator's eye, measuring everything it saw as a possible meal. It reminded me of Thompson. She swam in front of me and sounded, her dorsal fin slipping beneath my feet. I stopped swimming and treaded water, spinning, watching her circle, keeping her in sight.

I didn't like this at all. I was still miles from shore and there was no way home but to swim. This could be a very long night. Or a short one.

This shark looked determined to have me. There was an excitement in her movements as she circled. I watched for her to hunch her back. That would be the sign of imminent attack.

She orbited again, traveling slowly in a complete perimeter of vision. She was cautious. I watched the monster shark swim closer, feeling more calm than I had a right to feel. For some reason my fear had fled with the shark's approach. She was something tangible, a brutal opponent who intended me harm. I'd seen her kind before and knew what had to be done.

I planned to hit her with the bangstick the first time she came within range again. It was my only hope. If she made a determined attack, the .44 magnum would have little effect. The round would eventually kill her, but it wouldn't stop her from opening those terrible jaws and taking me with her. My only chance was to kill the shark before she attacked.

Suddenly she swam away, retreating to the extreme range of visibility. She was only a faint shadow, moving slowly, circling me. She was spooked and she wasn't afraid of me. Something else was out there. I wondered what could scare something the size of this monster. That potential wasn't something I wanted to contemplate.

If she had recently mated, the male might still be around. Sharks may be as promiscuous as Californians, but the males stay around for a few weeks. As big as she was, the male would be bigger. And more aggressive.

I started swimming again, slowly gliding with my best combat stroke, simultaneously looking in all directions, swiveling my head. I knew something was there, but I couldn't see it. I felt it, though. There was a feeling in the water of some massive presence.

The biggest shark I had ever seen swam directly in front of me, not fifteen feet away. He must have been tracking me for some time, hanging back, stalking the weak surface swimmer. This one looked bigger than twenty feet and it was probably the one that had eaten Jasmine. If so, it must have followed me from the time I'd been thrown into the water.

The beast circled once, getting the sense of what I was, and then closed in. There was no time to do anything but react. I hit the shark on the top of the head, just in front of the dorsal fin. The .44 magnum projectile and the expanding gases exploded through the brain chamber of the creature. The bullet exited the thorax, spewing blood and offal into the water. The giant shark shuddered, jinxed right and swam away, trailing bloody white strings of tissue. He started a wide circle, aimed back toward his original angle of attack and closed in.

I reloaded my last round, the surcharge of adrenaline overcoming the handicap of the cuffs.

The shark turned, exertion pumping black blood from its wounds, and came directly at me. I raised the bangstick, my last line of defense. It felt totally ineffectual, like aiming a camera at a charging elephant.

The shark hunched its back, his huge jaws open, teeth spread outward toward me, jagged horizontal armament leading the charge like lances. As he approached, he began to list to one side, as if my first shot had damaged some control mechanism somewhere deep in his prehistoric brain. Pectoral fins failed to stabilize him and he continued to roll, his great gaping mouth moving away from me. When he got close he hit me with the top of his head, shoving me back through the water. His jaws snapped shut and I could hear the crack of gristle like a hammer blow as lower and upper teeth slammed together. I rode the creature's snout, pinned against his dorsal fin while I was pushed backward through the water, his powerful tail pushing him onward toward an unknown destination.

I got my legs around the shark's body and dug in, trying to gain some balance so I could use my last round. I raised the bangstick and smashed it down against the head of the shark, just above the great eye. The bullet blew out the remainder of the brain case.

The great beast heeled over, turning away. I released my grip on the flanks of the shark and then I was violently shoved aside. The female tiger rocketed past me and hit the big wounded fish in the belly, tearing away a great mouthful of meat.

She had been behind the big shark, waiting for an opening. I'd lost sight of her while her mate attacked.

She turned in a tight circle that would have made an F-14 pilot proud and struck the other shark again, descending with it as the huge body spiraled into the depths, hitting the beast repeatedly until both animals were lost from sight.

So much for shark love.

I began swimming as carefully and as quietly as I could. The two sharks were deep and getting deeper every minute and I wanted to put as much distance as I could between them and me. I didn't know what else was out there.

I was so tired I almost didn't care.

$$\mathsf{YYYYYYYY}$$

21

Kate's voice was groggy and indistinct.

"Who is this?"

"It's John Caine."

"What do you want?"

Kate's was an uncharitable but understandable reaction to being awakened by a pager's call in the early morning hours. I didn't have her telephone number, but she had given me her beeper, and I tried it. It was a shot in the dark, but I needed help and I needed the kind of help she could provide. There were others I could have called, but she was keyed into this case and she would understand more quickly than most.

"Can you come get me?"

I could hear her moving around on the other end of the line, adjusting to the transition from sleep to wakefulness. As tired as I was, a transitory vision of what she might look like in her bed flashed across my mind. "Jesus! Do you know what time it is?"

"Midnight."

"Try three!"

"Didn't know. Sorry. I hate to bother you but you're the only one I know who has a key to handcuffs."

"Playing games? I didn't think you went for that kind of stuff."

"I don't."

There was a silence while she digested the tone of my voice. My answer had been much harsher than I'd intended.

"Are you in trouble?"

"I'm in handcuffs. I've been shot in the leg. I've been hit on the head and left for dead ten miles at sea. I just made it to shore. I'm at a pay phone near the lighthouse below Diamond Head. You know where it is?"

"Jesus! Do you need an ambulance?"

"I need to talk to you. I need clean clothes and I need a place to hide."

"Stay right there. I'll call for a uniform to get you out of the cuffs—"

"No! You come. I'll hide until I see your car."

"It's serious."

"As bone cancer," I said.

"Give me twenty minutes," she said and hung up.

The telephone booth had a light over it and it was working. I moved away from the light toward the kiawe scrub at the top of the cliff. Nothing moved. The night was balmy, but I was chilled by my swim and the loss of blood, and felt nauseous from the pain. The bullet wound had finally stopped bleeding while I was in the water but now it was welling blood again, slowly weeping what was left of my precious supply down the back of my leg.

I'd made it to shore without finding any more sharks, or having any more sharks find me. I kept the bangstick in my hand all the way. I still held it, a talisman. Even empty, it gave me a sense of security.

I squatted in the bushes and used the tip of my buckle knife to cut the poison sacs of the Portuguese man-of-war from my stomach and chest, where I could reach. I'd blundered into a

125

pod of jellyfish about a hundred yards from shore, just after crossing the reef. Hot burning pokers jabbing into my flesh cut through my exhaustion, hundreds of barbs lighting up all at once. My body was so close to total shutdown that all my circuits weren't reporting in. I ignored the pain and swam through them. I wasn't going back out *there!* Hundreds of long, piercing strings, tough as monofilament, wrapped my body. Only Portuguese man-of-war have those long, terrible tentacles. I jammed my mouth tight and screamed as quietly as I could. I screamed all the way to the beach.

I kept digging at my flesh until I saw the familiar lines of Kate's blue Mustang stop at the rock wall. She blinked her lights and I stepped out of the darkness.

"Jesus!"

"Just John," I said. I felt lightheaded, close to shock. I fought it, and kept fighting it. She opened the car door and I leaned in. "I'm going to mess up your upholstery." Blood trickled down my chest. More wounds had been opened by my digging out the jellyfish sacs.

"Just a minute." Kate spread a blue beach towel over the seat. It had the word HAWAII printed on it in black capital letters. I collapsed into the sports car.

She started asking questions but I smiled and held up my cuffed hands. "First things first," I said.

"From what I know about you that kind of fits. They should be in back, though."

"They were," I said. "I found a way to get them to the front."

She shook her head and unlocked the handcuffs. They fell to the carpet.

"Do you feel up to a little surgery?"

She shook her head. "You've got to see a doctor. You've been shot?"

"In the ass," I confirmed. "Or close enough. I can feel the bullet just under the skin. If you can pull it out and pour hydrogen peroxide in the wound I'm sure it'll be all right."

"Jesus!"

"Come on, Kate. You're supposed to be tough."

"Nothing like this!"

"I'll make you a deal. I'll tell you all about it if you get the bullet out and let me stay at your place."

She snorted. "That's your approach to lonely women at three in the morning? 'Hey, baby! If you let me come home with you I'll tell you a story and let you pull a bullet out of my ass!' No thank you."

"Do you have access to missing persons files?" I asked. "How about a plain blond girl, midteens, with a tattoo of a red heart on her right hip and keloid surgery scars on her right knee?"

"Carolyn Hammel. She's a missing person case. She's been on milk cartons. Where have you been?"

"I don't drink milk. I know what happened to her."

She eyed me intently, unblinking.

"You do." It was affirmation of my truth.

"I saw a video of her death. Two men who appeared to be Japanese nationals raped and murdered her and got it all on videotape as a souvenir. I think they're Japanese nationals—they spoke the language. I have reason to believe Thompson was the photographer. He claimed to be the producer. Said he had more of them, quote, nearly enough to retire, unquote. He showed me this film just before another little girl, the one you knew as Jasmine, was fed to the sharks off Makapu'u Point and I have reason to believe he filmed her death as a special order for a customer. I was tossed in after her but the sharks didn't like me."

"Close the door," she said.

"I can't go home."

"Close the door."

"I am not going to the hospital."

"Close the door, put on your seat belt and shut up," she ordered.

We spent the next ten minutes traveling through a dark and

silent Honolulu. Even Waikiki is quiet at three in the morning. But nothing matched the silence inside Kate's Mustang.

She pulled into the parking structure of her building and hustled me out of the car and into the elevator. I wore the bloody blue towel around my shoulders, my bare feet and sodden khaki trousers strikingly out of place in the Marco Polo, a high-rise condominium along the Ala Wai Canal. Kate's apartment was a one-bedroom unit facing the mountains.

"Do you want to shower?"

I nodded.

"Probably be best before. Get that salt off you. That way I can clean your wounds." She was pawing through her medicine cabinet. "Shit! Rubbing alcohol. No peroxide. Can I use alcohol? It'll burn like hell."

"Might as well," I said. "Everything else hurts."

"I'll look in the kitchen." She left the door open.

I undressed, shucking the towel and my wet trousers. I got a look at myself in the mirror. The Phrobis knife sheath was still strapped to my calf, and a single strand of duct tape adorned my upper thigh. Blood caked the hair behind my ear; the seawater hadn't completely dissolved the clot. My chest and arms were covered with long, wandering welts. My back still had tentacles and the purple poison sacs sticking to my skin. Blood ran freely down my leg and dripped on the tile floor. My eyes wore a haunted, exhausted look, the kind of expression you see on people who have raised the cover of hell and have taken a good, long look into one of the far corners. Most of the time they sleep in parks or on the street and ask you for money as you pass by. Most of them talk to themselves.

I leaned in and turned on the shower. I waited for the water to warm.

As I stood there on unsteady legs, Kate came in. She appraised my condition, ignoring my nakedness. Her appraisal was clinical. As tired as I was, I was still mildly disappointed.

"Jesus! Did they horsewhip you, too?"

128

"Jellyfish. You got any meat tenderizer?"

"I'll look."

She came back quickly with a small brown bottle. There was concern in her eyes I hadn't seen before. "Turn around." She had tweezers and a steak knife.

I turned around and leaned against the wall while she plucked the poison sacs from my back with the steak knife and picked them up with the tweezers, one by one. It was a slow, tedious process.

"Ouch! Shit! These things hurt!"

"I know," I said. I was used to the pain. I was surprised how well the body could adjust.

"You look bad. You're not going to go into shock or something? I don't want you dying on me."

I assured her I had no intention of either going into shock or dying. I wasn't about to survive the previous twelve hours just to die in her bathroom.

"I found some peroxide in the kitchen and I'm going to sacrifice a clean white sheet. I don't have many bandages here. I can get some in the morning, but these will have to do for now."

I stepped into the shower and closed the sliding glass door. "Thank you, Kate. I mean it." She offered no response. She stood there, staring at me through the frosted glass for a moment, then she turned and left the bathroom.

I removed the tape and the knife sheath and finished my shower, avoiding the places where there were holes in my hide. That covered a lot of territory. The soap stung the raw flesh. The water hurt the jellyfish stings. Kate came back with clean towels and helped me climb out, then dried me gently. The towels felt as if they'd been kept in the oven. Even after the warm shower I still felt chilled.

When she finished drying me the towels were streaked red with my blood.

"Jesus, you look bad," she said, her voice low with concern.

"Come here." She led me to her bedroom where she had prepared her surgery. A bright tensor desk lamp was positioned over the sheet, the bedclothes turned back. Tweezers, towels and other implements were professionally laid out on a nearby table. "Lie down," said Kate. It was a command.

I lay facedown on the bed, staring out the window at the lights of Manoa and the University of Hawaii across the valley. The thought of being stretched out naked on Kate's bed at four in the morning had never occurred to me. If it had, the present circumstances would not have been in that particular fantasy.

"Tell me everything," she ordered as she began working on the bullet wound. "I'll try not to hurt you, John, but I don't see how that's possible."

While she worked I told her everything, even the things I'd planned on withholding. You can't very well lie to a woman who is pulling a bullet out of your backside. You have to trust her. She finished and put a dressing on the wound. I heard the clink of heavy metal falling into a glass.

"Two-twenty-three Remington," she said. "You'd probably call it a five point five–six millimeter. I've sent a few bullets to the lab before but this is the first one I've ever removed from the victim myself. No problem with the chain of evidence here. Right from your butt to the bag. If we can find the weapon we'll get a match. No distortion, either. I thought you were tough."

"The water cut the velocity. I haven't got to that part of the story yet."

"Go ahead. I'm going to work on your scalp now. Is there a bullet in there, too? If you shake your head will it rattle?"

"No. Somebody hit me from behind. I haven't got to that part, either."

"Should I be recording this?"

"No. Listen to the whole story. Then we'll decide what to do."

"We? I don't think so. This is out of your hands now. I'll decide what to do."

"Once you've heard the story. Hear me out."

She moved to the other side of the bed and began working on my head wound. "Let me see your eyes," she said. Painfully I raised my head while she checked the pupils. "Doesn't look like a concussion, but you've got about an inch of scalp gone back there." She cleaned the wound and made concerned sounds deep in her throat.

When she finished, she handed me a robe and I followed her to the living room. We sat on the couch while I finished my story. There was a feeling of intimacy I hadn't noticed before. Kate made coffee and microwaved croissants from her freezer. They tasted good, but food did not appeal. I ate them covered with strawberry preserves. I know I had burned a huge amount of calories and they needed replenishment. She made me drink a lot of water. I was thirsty and obeyed.

Kate was an excellent listener. She paid attention to more than just words. She watched my face and listened with her whole being. She did not take notes but I knew she would remember the salient facts, and I understood that she was comparing and processing what she heard with what she already knew. Kate was a homicide detective, a good one, and she was working.

By the time my story was finished the coffeepot was empty, the croissants were gone and the sun was warming the Ko'olau Mountains above Manoa. I'd been awake for twenty-six hours. My eyes felt gritty.

"I've got to get to work," said Kate. "I want to talk to my boss about this and I want to pull the files on the girl you saw. I want a positive ID. I'll also bring home some other missing persons files and Jane Does that turned up last year.

"If it's any consolation, this was what I had heard rumored about Thompson. The snuff films. You've corroborated the story I got earlier this year. Only I knew about it from a confidential informant."

"Whom do I corroborate?"

"It doesn't matter now. The witness is dead."

Choy. It had to be. The boy had been doing all kinds of back-channel work, getting money anywhere he could. I admired his energy, if not his judgment.

"I'll lock up and you can use my bed. Can you sleep?"

"I don't think I can do anything else," I admitted.

YYYYYYYY

22

I huddled in the middle of Kate's bed surrounded by pink cotton ruffles. I pretended sleep, hopeful she would mistake my deep, regular breathing for the real thing. She didn't. I listened as a dresser drawer opened and closed, and then I heard her bathroom door close and lock. Her liberal attitude about nudity apparently wasn't mutual. I closed my eyes.

The next time I looked at her bedroom clock it was nearly noon. Kate hadn't turned on the air conditioning and I was suffocating beneath the pink ruffles. I turned down the covers and carefully rolled over.

"I'd like to say I'm impressed but I don't think that's for me."

I opened my eyes.

The bedclothes were on the floor. I was flat on my back, uncovered and sporting a rock-hard erection. Kate stood at the foot of the bed, smiling a tired smile.

I rolled onto my stomach.

"The man's shy."

"The man hurts," I moaned. It was true. Every part of my

body was stiff, sore or on fire. My muscles were sore. My thigh throbbed from the gunshot wound. The back of my head pounded like the all-time world record hangover. I smelled like meat loaf. The meat tenderizer had taken some of the fire away, but not all of it. That pain wouldn't go away for days.

"I don't know who you were dreaming about, but it was an impossible dream," she said. "You look like you might die if somebody touched you."

She was right. *Air* hurt.

She covered my body with a sheet. "I forgot to turn on the air conditioning when I left. I'm sorry." Her voice was tender and solicitous. I nearly didn't recognize it.

"I don't remember dreaming."

"It's okay, cowboy. You don't have to tell me."

"I have no secrets from you, Kate."

"Yeah. Ain't that the truth." She sat on the bed, close to me but not touching, as if I were a patient with an exotic, contagious disease. "Do you feel up to thinking? I've been working on this all day and I think I've got enough to go on."

"Go where?"

"My boss thinks we have enough for a warrant. We'll hit the boat and his house. With your sworn statement we can get—"

"I'm not giving anybody a sworn statement."

"But you said—"

"Kate. Remember what I'm in this for?"

"Yes, but—"

"I need to clear MacGruder's daughter."

"But she's dirty!"

"She's dead! And she was killed because she objected to killing little girls! Getting her involved now will only destroy an innocent man and it won't hurt Thompson at all. We'll get Thompson. And you'll put him out of business. But we'll have to do it my way."

"Too late," she said. She glanced at her watch. It was a bit

134

of action for me to follow. Because I had been injured I was supposed to be slow and stupid, too. "There's a team on its way to *Pele* right now."

I smiled. "There won't be any tapes, any incriminating evidence of any kind on that boat. Except a hole in the hull."

"How can you be so sure?"

"Thompson wouldn't leave anything to chance. He would not leave anything like that on a boat that is going to have service people aboard. I put a hell of a hole in the bottom of *Pele*. She won't be going anywhere until that's repaired. He's reckless in some ways but he won't leave those tapes lying around. They'll either be at his home or in another location we don't know about, a safe house."

"What is this thing?" She held up the UM-1. I'd forgotten about it, and must have left it in her Mustang. For the first time I told her about the sharks. She shook her head. "You've got more lives than a cat! Jesus!"

"Wish I were Jesus," I said. "I could have walked on water."

"But you know what happened to him, don't you?"

"Couldn't hurt worse than I do now."

"Get some rest. I'm waiting for the call. You hungry?"

"Starved." That surprised me. I thought I was too tired to eat.

"I brought some hot and sour soup from Wo Fat's. That sound good?"

Chinese penicillin. I admitted that it sounded good and it made me think of an old man in Chinatown with a dead son and a dead concubine and a contract on John Caine. He had sacrificed his son for reasons too obscure for me to follow. He had played strange games with more people than I would have thought possible and for the most unfathomable of reasons.

This whole case was full of people taking the lives of others for questionable reasons and I was getting a little sick of it.

I knew the raiding team would come up empty. Thompson would like to believe he had killed me, but he wouldn't be sure and he couldn't leave it to chance. He was so certain he would kill me that he ran off at the mouth and told me too much. If I were Thompson I'd have somebody watch *Duchess* to see if I turned up. And I'd make preparations for early retirement. I didn't see him making any more videos until he was certain I'd become shark bait. That made some unknown young girls safe for a while. At least from that predator.

He must have some nagging doubts about me. I couldn't imagine what had gone through his mind when the .44 slug rocketed up from the bilge.

I smiled at the thought.

Kate returned with the soup. I sat up, covering myself as well as I could.

"Don't bother," she said. "I've seen it all."

"Can you call off the boat search? I mean, is it really too late?"

"What do you mean?"

"I just thought if Thompson thinks I'm dead it could be useful to both of us. Raiding that boat is a tipoff that I survived. He'd know."

She thought about it. She'd had a long day and night and it showed. I could see dark circles under her eyes. Even exhausted she was still beautiful, easy on my eyes. After all the horror of the day before, being with her was like finding a peaceful island with a safe harbor.

"It could be useful," she said carefully, as if she were realizing the fact of the words as she uttered them.

"Can you turn it off?"

"I can try," she said, making up her mind. Her eyes flashed twin smiles at me, mischievous dimples appearing on her face. Twenty years dropped and I could see her as she had been as a little girl. "I'm going to use you, John Caine. You might not like it, but I'm going to use you."

"A guy could get used to it," I said, wondering what she had in mind.

23

"You might think you're doing something creative here, Mr. Caine, but you are nothing but an interloper. This is strictly a matter for law enforcement. You don't belong in this." Kate's boss, Captain Dale Yoshida, loomed over me as well as he could. He was a thin, nervous nisei in a dark blue suit, white shirt and black knit tie. He was barely five feet tall. His cigarette-roughened, movie-tough's voice made him seem taller than he really was. He reminded me of a Japanese version of Humphrey Bogart.

I slumped in Kate's leather chair, dressed in freshly washed khakis and a black and green Aloha shirt she'd purchased for me. I was still barefoot.

"You wanna give us a statement or be held as a material witness? What's it gonna be?"

"Neither," I said. "Let me go over it one more time."

"Forget that. We're not taking any suggestions from you. What do you do for a living? Private detective?"

I nodded. "Most of my work is executive protection and asset recovery." Asset recovery was a fancy name for retrieving stolen property. Because of the volume, that made up the bulk of my income. I liked the way the buzzwords sounded as they rolled off my tongue.

"Whatever. Tell me again how you got messed up in this?"

"I'm doing inquiries for Admiral Winston MacGruder, the father of the murdered girl. The trail led me to Thompson." Well okay, it wasn't the truth, the whole truth and nothing but the truth, but this wasn't a priest I was talking to.

Yoshida glared at Kate, who was sitting on her couch, her legs curled underneath her body. Her posture and her poise were utterly feminine. Her face betrayed nothing.

"This clown licensed?"

"Yes. And he's known to HPD and DEA. Talk to Lieutenant Kahanamoku. He checked him out. According to DEA and Kimo he's loose, but he's straight."

Yoshida grunted and turned back to me.

"You claim you saw a videotape of a girl being raped and murdered by two Japanese nationals. You subsequently identified the victim in the movie as Carolyn Hammel. And you claim the owner of the motor vessel *Pele* then murdered his receptionist, a girl named Jasmine, whom we both know works for Chawlie Choy, by feeding her to the sharks. And you claim that he threw you into the sea, right after that attack, and you managed to fight off the sharks and swim ten miles to shore in the middle of the night. You expect me to believe all that?"

"That's what happened."

"But you won't give us a formal statement."

"No, sir."

Yoshida looked through his notes. "You claimed that you were fired on while you were in the water. With automatic weapons. Oh, and I like this. They handcuffed you and strapped a heavy weight belt on you before they threw you in. And you escaped. Who're you, Houdini?"

"I got lucky."

"Yeah." He let the silence continue for a few heartbeats to underscore his disbelief, his eyes never leaving mine. "You claim they fired on you while you were in the water and one of the rounds struck you in the leg. You returned fire. You

138

admit to firing a forty-four-caliber round from this"—Yoshida held up my UM-1—"into the bottom of the hull, driving off the boat."

"That's correct."

"You admit to all that."

"Yes, sir."

"You admit to an act of piracy on the high seas, a federal crime. Is that how you want me to charge you?"

I said nothing. I couldn't tell if Captain Yoshida was serious or if he were testing me. I decided he was too smart to actually believe what he was saying.

"Let me go over this part again. You admit to giving information to Thompson, this alleged criminal, about a man in his organization, one Garrick Choy. And this man subsequently was found tortured and shot to death in a cane field near Waipahu. You claim that this information was given to you by the man's father, who knew what you were going to do with the information. Is that right?"

"It isn't right, but it's what happened."

"This isn't the time for humor, Mr. Caine. Is what I said accurate? Did the father of this boy intentionally set him up for murder through you, as unwilling or as unwitting as you claim to have been?"

"At the time, Garrick Choy was being held by some of Chawlie's people at his home. Garrick escaped and ran straight to Thompson. We didn't know until after it happened."

"You know for a fact that he escaped on his own? Without help? Or was he set free?"

I shook my head. "I have some ideas on the subject, but you wouldn't be interested."

"It sounds pretty fucking far-fetched to me," said Yoshida.

Except it was the truth. I was grateful that Yoshida had keyed on the facts I'd presented in the order I'd presented them. He'd stayed away from Mary MacGruder, whose involvement in the torture films was known to Kate. And I was gratified that Kate had not told Yoshida about Thompson's blackmail approach to the admiral, or MacGruder's apparent failure to report it.

MacGruder may have known who murdered his daughter when he hired Souza.

"What about this Jeep that's been impounded over at Young Street? It was left with its motor running and the keys in the ignition in the middle of an intersection. It's registered to you. You want to report it stolen? Or you want to admit to abandoning your vehicle?"

"I'll admit to all of that."

"You're gonna have trouble getting insurance in this state, you know that?" Yoshida turned over another page of his notebook. "I can't decide whether to charge you with abandonment of a motor vehicle or with reckless endangerment, or with interfering with a police investigation. That's a felony. I think I can make it stick, too."

When I did not respond, he continued.

"On the basis of Detective Alapai's report, which was based almost entirely upon two confidential informants, we acquired a federal search warrant and detailed a raiding party to the Honolulu Yacht Club this afternoon. Before we got there we were forced to call it off because our star witness—you—refused to cooperate. The other CI is dead. And if I'm to understand your statement made willingly to Detective Alapai, you gave the information to his killers as to his activities, which directly resulted in his death. And you're supposed to be my witness?"

"I'm not your witness," I said.

"You're anything I want you to be, Caine. We have no evidence a crime has been committed, except the ones you admit to. Did you know that even if we had that fucking tape in our possession, even with a clear chain of evidence, we might not get a conviction in a court of law? Tapes are being thrown out of court right and left these days. Photographs, motion pictures and videotapes are becoming inadmissible as evidence more and more. They're too easily changed by computers.

"So you saw a tape. So what? Hollywood does it all the time. They make it look real. It's their job, remember? And the receptionist, Jasmine? What's her real name?"

"I don't know."

"Did you actually see her thrown to the sharks? Did you witness her murder?"

"No."

"No. So you cannot give evidence that anyone else was even on that boat, much less thrown to the sharks. She could have been a prop, this whole thing just a charade to fool you."

"I don't think so." I remembered the bruises on her arms and legs and I remembered the terror in her eyes. Nothing had been faked. And they had been fairly serious about trying to kill me.

"You don't think so." Yoshida's eyes bored into me, searching for the lie.

"But it happened," I said, holding my stare.

Yoshida nodded.

"Yeah," he said. "I know it did."

Behind Yoshida, Kate sat up on the couch and put her feet on the carpet, listening intently.

"This afternoon the Shark Task Force caught an eighteen-foot tiger shark off Sandy Beach. It vomited the contents of its stomach when it was brought aboard the boat. The crew found pieces of what looked to be the lower portion of a human torso. It had not been in the shark's stomach for long. Medical examiner's got it now, but it had been identified as a human female, twenty to twenty-five years of age. The time of death is impossible to determine, as is a positive identification. We're getting DNA typing but we need something to compare to.

"We have a missing person report on Thompson's secretary by her roommates. I've got a team of lab people going through her bathroom. They're looking for hair samples and they might have to resort to her toothbrush for dried saliva. We might get lucky.

"Your story will be verified."

"But the shark I killed was a twenty-footer."

Yoshida shrugged. "There's plenty of them to go around out there," he said. "One or two less doesn't bother me. Then there's the two-twenty-three Remington slug that Jane Wayne over there pulled out of your, ah, your leg. It's impossible to shoot yourself in the butt with a high-powered rifle without having traumatic injury so severe your leg would have to be amputated. And there would be powder burns. I've discussed your wound, as Detective Alapai described it, and the condition of the bullet with the medical examiner. He told me that your wound and the bullet's lack of impairment are totally consistent with your version of the events. Therefore, I'm willing to believe almost everything you've told us.

"You've confirmed what Kate's original confidential informant told her. We've suspected Thompson has been producing snuff films for over six months, but we can't find any victims and we can't find any real evidence that he's actually doing it. Other than the Hammel girl and the MacGruder woman, no bodies or even a trace of the crime have surfaced. From what you told me I think I know how he's getting rid of the bodies. And from what I know of sharks I think I know why the sudden increase in the number of large tigers and whites off our shores, and the increase in the number of shark attacks here."

I nodded, waiting for what must be coming next.

"But that doesn't mean anything to us right now. We've got a one-man crime wave out there. Two, if we count you. But we've nothing to take to a grand jury for indictment. Thompson can leave the island any time he wants. I can't stop him. He can continue what he's been doing and I can't do anything about it. I wish you'd shot him, but no such luck. Our sources told us he got off the boat, him and all his boys. Nobody seems to have been hurt."

"Only murdered," I said. I didn't count. I was getting my strength back. The gunshot wound was actually just a small puncture wound, no worse than I would have received sitting on a nail. The jellyfish stings were painful, but getting less so every hour. And the bump on my head didn't give me a concussion. My real physical problem was exhaustion and blood loss. With sleep and a decent meal or two I'd be running again. In a day or two.

"Yeah. It looks that way."

"If you can find that AR-15 you can match the bullet. The one Kate took out of my leg."

"Chances are he ditched it at sea before he reached the harbor."

I agreed. That's what I would have done, given the circumstances of a possible miss and a flooding bilge, and the remote possibility of a police reception at the dock. The tapes would have gone overboard, too. Those were copies, of course. The masters would be carefully hidden. That set my mind working in another direction.

"Kate suggested that we could use you. Thompson thinks he's won, but he's not sure. In a day or two, if you don't show up at your boat, he'll know it. Lay low for a couple of days. Rest up. Let your wounds heal. We'll keep it our secret that you're still alive. Just the three of us. I don't want to hear that some Chinese criminal knows you're still breathing. In a few days we'll talk and decide what to do."

I nodded. But I already knew what I was going to do.

"No official reports. No nothing. That way Kate doesn't get in trouble for practicing medicine without a license and not reporting a gunshot wound to the police."

"I am the police, Dale." She hadn't said much so far because her boss was talking to me.

Yoshida glanced over his shoulder and grinned. "Yeah.

That's right. I almost forgot." He turned back to me, the grin on his face fading as he turned. "Kate's CI report will be buried. You're a missing person as of tonight. Or you would be if someone cared enough about you to report you missing. Do you have anyone who would miss you, Caine, if you were to vanish?"

I thought about it. It didn't take long.

"No," I said. "I don't have anybody."

VVVVVVVV

24

Kate walked Yoshida to the door. I remained where I was, partly because they wanted to talk about me where I couldn't hear what they had to say and partly because it hurt too much to move. They stopped in her tiny kitchen and spoke quietly for a few minutes before he patted her shoulder and stumped out the door. I noted that before he left he took something from his pocket and handed it to Kate.

She set the double locks on the door and went into her bedroom, telling me that she needed a shower and a change of clothes. I sat in the easy chair and watched a rainsquall passing over the mountains, waiting for the rainbow I knew would follow, and listening to the sounds of the woman in her bathroom. It was a private and intimate scene, the kind of thing I'd seldom experienced. I kept my eyes on the mountains and my ears attuned to the sounds coming from the bathroom, appreciating for a time the softer things in life.

Kate returned from her shower and sat next to me, bringing a glass of wine for each of us. She handed me my keys. I weighed them in my palm.

"I've been forgiven of my sins?"

She nodded, smiling. "It would seem so." She was wearing a pink silk robe over matching silk pajamas, like the ones they used to wear in old movies. It made her look like a Polynesian Lauren Bacall. Her manner had transformed during Yoshida's visit. She'd become proprietary. It made me feel a little uncomfortable, yet I liked it.

I'm not used to being owned or having anyone even make the claim. I'm a single, not any part of a couple. It is difficult to remember a time when it's been any other way. I'd been attracted to Kate when I first met her and I thought she only tolerated my company in return. This was different.

"You really don't have anyone, do you?" she asked.

"No. I live alone. I work alone."

"Never married?"

"Well . . ." I said, thinking this was not the time to drag out old lost loves.

"Go ahead," said Kate. "Tell me about her."

"Almost married," I said. "I met a girl in junior high school and fell in love with her immediately. It was like I'd been hit with a lightning bolt. Her name was Jayne, with a *y*, and she suddenly became the only female that existed on the planet. Other girls seemed to be of a different species."

"This was junior high school?"

"Classic case of first love. I was thirteen. She was twelve. She couldn't see anything good in me until high school so I carried the torch by myself. It didn't dim, either, and she eventually came around. Maybe I grew up a little. Maybe she saw through what I was on the surface and realized that I really loved her, I don't know, but we became a couple. We went together all through high school and college. Every year it was John and Jayne or Jayne and John. We were inseparable.

"This was the midsixties, you'll remember, although you might be too young to remember what those times were all about. It was a time of free love, drugs and attacking the establishment. We weren't like that. While other kids were taking their clothes off, smoking dope on street corners and protesting the war, we were planning for a future together, saving our money and making plans for the house with the white picket fence, two children and a dog.

"We agreed that I'd graduate from college, join the navy and marry when I got out, or at least not until I was given a permanent duty station. We chose the navy because the Vietnam War was in full swing then and it seemed to be the safest branch of service available.

"I studied hard. I got straight As. Because of Jayne. I didn't want to let her down. I graduated and was accepted to OCS. I worked hard there to turn myself into the best officer possible. Because I grew up on the water I excelled at what the navy called basic seamanship, and I was a whiz at the books. It sounds as though I'm bragging but it was true. I applied myself harder than I'd ever applied myself before. I ranked third in my class and was closing in on the second spot, right behind an Eastern establishment type from Harvard.

"So it was difficult to understand why I was called to the commanding officer's office, pulled from morning inspection. Two marines all but arrested me and brought me to his office without any explanation.

"I was told, as politely and as gently as that kind of news could be told, that Jayne had been run down by a drunken driver in a crosswalk at six-thirty in the morning the day before. She'd been dead a whole day before anyone thought to notify me. The driver had been drinking all night and ran the red light because he said he didn't see it—the sun was in his eyes. He didn't see the young woman in the crosswalk, either. He had no explanation why he'd been driving seventy miles an hour in a twenty-five-mile zone.

"I was informed that I could be relieved of my duties at the school for a temporary pass to attend the funeral. The co told me that he'd see I was treated fairly. She wasn't immediate family, you see. Not yet. I believed him. He was a good man, and I sincerely believed that he would do as he promised, but there was nothing back home now for me to go to. Jayne was gone and I was alone. I thanked him and told him I'd stay. He must have thought I was a cold bastard.

"It struck me that for that whole day after her death she'd still been alive to me, as alive as she'd ever been during our separation. I don't know what significance that had, but I wondered about it for years afterward. I finally decided it's always like that. Until you get confirmation, someone's still alive. So don't push confirmation. Avoid it at all cost.

"I graduated second in my class. Ahead of the Harvard guy and right behind a guy who'd been in the navy for years, who'd been a senior enlisted noncom before. Nobody came to my graduation."

Kate looked at me strangely. "You didn't go to the funeral?"

"No. Funerals are only for those left behind. Even then I thought them too public. My parents were both dead. I had the grief, but I didn't have anyone to share it with. I held my own private ceremony for her. It's only important when you remember the person who has gone."

"Have you been in love since?"

"In lust a couple of times."

Kate's hands gently cradled my face, turning my gaze from the window until our noses were almost touching. I looked deeply into her eyes. "You've never told that story to anyone before, have you?"

"Nobody ever asked . . ."

She kissed my forehead and released me. My scalp tingled where she touched me. "You are a strange man, John Caine. Is that why you became a SEAL?"

"Yeah."

"Because you wanted to test yourself?"

"Nothing like that. They were the best and I wanted to be the best."

"You still love her."

"I always will."

Kate got up and refilled my glass. I didn't remember draining it. She poured herself another, too, killing the bottle. "We haven't discussed sleeping arrangements," she said, her voice husky. "Since you're the invalid you'll take the bed. It's comfortable and you'll sleep better there. I'll sleep on the couch.

"I get up every morning at five-thirty and I run for thirty minutes. While I'm gone you can shower. When I come back the bathroom is mine. All mine. For an hour. It's my time of the day. Coffee is on a timer. Any questions?"

"Thank you, Kate. This has been an unexpected surprise."

"For what? Taking the lead out of your butt?"

"No," I said, smiling. "For taking me in."

She reached across the space between us and patted my hand. "I realized I could trust you. You're one of the few men I've known who hasn't lied to me, or who hasn't tried to use me or use my position. I haven't known you long, but I know you well. I trust you. And I guess I realized that we've been friends all along and I didn't know it."

VVVVVVV

25

I had a difficult time getting to sleep. I couldn't find a comfortable position in the bed. Any way I turned hurt something. But it wasn't because of my injuries alone. Thoughts of Kate on her couch intruded. Memory of her touch lingered. I replayed the views I'd had of her face in profile. I recalled every word of our conversation. Eventually I drifted off, dreaming of pink silk pajamas.

I woke as weight was applied to the mattress, still in the dream I was having just before waking. Kate, dressed in pink silk, had been trying to tell me something. I couldn't understand what she wanted no matter how much I tried. We were both frustrated. I opened my eyes.

Kate, minus the pink pajamas, was crouched beside the bed. In the light-shadowed darkness I saw her breasts sway sweetly as she leaned over to open the covers.

I was in the middle of the bed, deep in the valley Kate's body had made from her single nights on the old mattress. I rolled to one side, accepting her embrace.

"Does this hurt?" she asked, touching me.

"Yes," I said. "Don't stop."

"Don't make anything out of this, okay?"

I looked at her face. It was lovely to watch her eyes looking back into mine. I never thought I'd see that look again on any woman's face.

"Sure," I said. "It means nothing."

Her hands explored my skin, skirting the wounds and the welts. I let her take the lead, allowing her anything she wanted. Her touch was gentle, as if she were afraid I might break. Ignoring the pain was not difficult. Most of it came from the welts and was of no consequence. I concentrated on the pleasure of touching another human being, a sensation lost for so long I'd nearly forgotten what it was like.

She became more demanding and I responded. This first time can be a clumsy affair, seldom satisfying to either party, but it wasn't that way for us. There was no urgency to join as we found the little places to linger. The longer we delayed, the better the anticipation.

Neither of us worried about my injuries.

She directed us, made me lie on my back and mounted me. The soft, sliding pleasure of it brought both of us to the brink, caused her to stiffen, then soften again. I looked up at her face, beautiful now that all protection had fallen. Tears were silently flowing down her cheeks. I held her as she began rocking to her own drumbeat, dancing to that most ancient of rhythms.

She stepped up the tempo of her dance, racing something inside of her, reaching for and finally grasping what she had been chasing. I followed, allowing her the freedom to take us wherever she wanted to go.

She collapsed on top of me. She felt me still inside of her and understood at once that I hadn't followed her over the edge.

She smiled. It was the mischievous grin I'd seen before.

"Nice guys finish last, huh?"

"Something like that," I said.

We rolled over as one, face to face, and moving inside of her I found myself hypnotized by her eyes. Our mouths came together, mirroring that other joining. Now I followed my own path and Kate found the rhythm and followed. This time we arrived at the same place at the same time. I made it a point to look into her eyes when it happened, watching her face. It increased my pleasure to watch her pleasure.

Icing on the cake.

Afterward we lay together, still joined. Her arms reached around me, holding me tightly to her as if I would float away if she didn't hold me down. I held her head, stroking her fine black hair, still watching her face. It made me think of rainbows. I am a confessed rainbow junkie. Each one is different, and I could stand and watch the brilliant pastels for hours if they'd last. I get a foolish smile on my face when I look at them. I felt the same way about Kate's face. It made me feel peaceful and happy.

She stiffened and released me.

"My God, doesn't that hurt?"

"What?"

"Touching your skin?"

I thought about it. I hadn't been aware of any pain. Now that she mentioned it, there was some, but it wasn't much. "Nothing that's not worth what I'm getting in return."

She hugged me again. Gently.

"You're a very strange man," she said again. "You're smart, smart enough to be president of General Motors. Yet you live out here and do nothing."

"I never could have been president of General Motors," I said. "They wouldn't have me and I wouldn't want them. I'm too independent and I can't eat that much shit or kiss that much ass. Jayne has nothing to do with what I do now. And what I do is not nothing. Long ago I decided there had to be someone who will not bend over and take it. There had to be someone people can turn to for justice when all other routes have been closed to them. Someone not connected to the bureaucratic machinery that inhibits it."

Still inside of Kate, I brushed the hair from her eyes.

"You make it sound so noble," she said. "Yet you described yourself as a retriever."

"Some parts of it are noble. Most of it is not."

"What happened to the man who killed her?" Kate's eyes bored into mine. I was keenly aware of her skills, and just as aware that we were still physically connected to each other. This was neither a time nor a place for sliding the truth.

"He died," I said.

She stared at me, expecting more.

"What did the courts do?"

"Gave him a suspended sentence. He was a thirty-year man in the navy, a senior chief. He'd been through World War Two and Korea. They didn't want to ruin his career."

The silence built. Kate could put two and two together faster than most.

"You killed him," she said after a while, her voice a quiet indictment.

"You don't want to know."

"There's no statute of limitations—"

"Don't ask questions of me if you don't want to know the answers. I'll tell you everything."

"I have to know, John."

I kissed her eyes. Tears trickled from their corners. I licked the tear tracks, tasting her salt.

"You know. That's enough."

She nodded and held me tightly to her, and wept.

Sometime in the night we found each other again, our bodies melding together as if we had been lovers for years and not hours. I took the lead this time, waiting for Kate to find her source of joy once, twice, three times before I shifted our bodies so we could come together. And we did, bodies clasped, two organic machines in harmonic rhythm, two sets of eyes fixed upon the other, two hungry mouths responding to identical needs. I spent myself into her as she writhed against me, calling my name through the kiss.

We didn't talk afterward. Kate nestled inside my arms, protected from the world by my body. My face was buried against her hair. I finally fell off the end of the world smelling her scent, feeling no pain at all. Of any kind.

VVVVVVVV

26

I woke again when Kate got out of bed. Early morning light filtered through the blinds. She closed the bathroom door, but did not lock it.

I lay awake and calculated that I'd spent nearly thirty hours in this apartment. By now Thompson should be convinced I had drowned, died of a gunshot wound or been eaten by sharks. I'd have to give it another day to be certain the watchers were called off. Until I was ready to make my move I couldn't risk going outside. Even with a population of nearly a million souls, Oahu is a tiny island. You'll run into the people you know everywhere you go. It's like a small town in that respect. It's nice, running into friends. If you make an enemy, you'll keep running into that person too. I'm convinced that's one of the reasons why people are so friendly in Hawaii. The Aloha Spirit is the child of necessity. You can't go anywhere else. You can't hide within the crowd as you can in a city on the mainland. There's a crowd here, but the faces are all too familiar.

If I went out, the chances were good that one of Thompson's people might see me. Thompson might not run if he thought I was dead. But if he knew I was alive there was no predicting what he might do. It would be more difficult and dangerous to approach him.

Which was just what I planned on doing when I felt a little better.

I needed some things off *Duchess* but there was no way I could get to them. My boat would be safe at the marina, even from Thompson's people. I could get along without anything as long as I remained here but once I started moving around again my needs would be more complicated.

I decided to keep it simple and stay where I'd been told to stay.

Kate came out of the bathroom, a towel in front of her, another turbaned in her hair. "I'm going for my run. How do you feel?" She came to the bed and kissed me and the towel fell away.

"I feel wonderful," I said, and it was true.

"You'll be all right?"

I assured her I was fine and sat back to watch her dress. It had been a long time since a woman had been so comfortable with me she felt she could dress in my presence. It had a familiar intimacy I liked and had missed.

She tied her shoes. "Don't go out for any reason. I'll bring a morning paper back with me." She kissed me again. "Coffee's ready when you want some."

She unlocked the door and was gone.

I got out of bed and tried my exercises. Putting my feet on the chair for my push-ups made the top of my head feel like someone was hitting me behind the ear with a hammer. I tried sit-ups and found they strained my leg and sent stabs of white pain that went right off the dolorometer. I decided to let my body rest for a couple of days.

I showered, mindful of Kate's warning that the bathroom was her sole territory when she returned. She had been explicit and I respected her honesty.

I was drying off, patting my skin rather than rubbing, when

she came back carrying a newspaper and humming something from *South Pacific*. She smiled at me, dark eyes flashing, communicating her feelings across the room. She stripped off her sweaty clothes and hung them on a wicker frame near the open window, then went to the kitchen. It gave me pleasure to watch her walk across the room, her lithe figure sparkling with sweat. She seemed so healthy her skin glowed.

"You take anything in your coffee?" Kate's voice floated from the kitchen. I was still rooted in the same place I'd been standing when she'd come bounding into the room, so full of energy even inanimate objects such as the furniture soaked up her vitality.

"No."

She returned to the bedroom bearing two steaming mugs. I couldn't take my eyes from her body while she set the mugs on the dresser.

"It's all yours," I said, meaning the bathroom.

She smiled and turned to me.

"It's all yours," she replied, spreading her arms toward me. I knew what she meant. I stood closer to her, inhaling her fragrance. Her perspiration had a sweet tang to it. It made me want to taste it.

"You're going to make me late for work," she murmured.

I knelt in front of her, my hands against the backs of her thighs, feeling smooth muscles tighten beneath my palms. "How many times have you been late for work?"

There was a silence, as if she were actually considering the question.

"Not once," she said. "Not yet." And she pressed her body to my hungry mouth.

"If I jump into the shower right now and hurry I might even make it," said Kate, glancing toward her clock radio.

I rolled away as she bounded across the bedroom into the bathroom, leaving the door open.

I heard the shower door open and close and the spray start. She squealed from the shock of the cold water. She'd be out of the shower before the water warmed. Feeling silly padding naked around her place, I put on the white robe and took the coffee mugs to the kitchen, poured the cold coffee down the sink and refilled both mugs.

When I came back to the bedroom she was already out of the shower. I handed her a cup.

"Thanks," she said, and took a quick sip and set it down. "Ouch! Hot!" She began dressing. I watched every snap, every roll of the nylon.

"I'm not sure you're good for me," she said. "Yes! I am sure. You might hurt my career but you're good for me!" She ran back to the bathroom.

She came out five minutes later, completely dressed, her hair and makeup in place. There was no hint she'd been engaged in physical pleasures less than fifteen minutes before. I was impressed and a little disappointed.

"Don't leave the apartment for any reason!" she said, grabbing her purse and briefcase.

"Yes, ma'am."

"I mean it."

"Don't forget your coffee," I said, feeling like a housewife.

She took the mug, kissed me and closed the door. All the energy left the apartment. I took off the robe and took another shower. I shampooed my hair and face. This was the second day I hadn't shaved and there was the beginning of heavy beard growth. I found a pink plastic razor and scraped my face as well as I could, using shampoo as shaving cream. I was careful but I cut myself twice. More of my already depleted blood supply leaked down the drain.

That was going to have to stop or I'd be nearly white from loss of blood.

I decided to call Max. It was time to let him know what had been going on and to ask for his help. Just a little help, nothing serious to get him in trouble. There were some things I wanted off *Duchess,* some things I'd feel better about having with me once I left the confines of my mink-lined prison. If Max didn't know someone who could get on and off my boat without being seen, the navy had become seriously deficient since my tenure.

A young voice with a heavy Southern drawl answered the telephone, giving me the unit identification and warning me that it was not a secure line.

"This is John Caine. Is Senior Chief White available?"

"Yes, sir. He said to connect you as soon as you called. Can you hold, sir?"

"Of course."

I didn't have to wait long.

"John. I heard you had some trouble."

"Not much. I know what I need to know. The first part of the operation is over." I sketched out the basics of what I'd learned, partly for him, partly for me. "I'm in hiding now, getting my strength back."

"I heard you got shot again."

"You've got a source at HPD?"

"Same leg, I heard," he replied, not answering my question.

"It's got a lead magnet, Max. Nothing serious."

"What do you need?"

"A face-to-face would be nice."

"Can't do that right now. Two days."

"A couple pints of blood wouldn't hurt, then."

"What can I really do for you?"

I decided not to reveal the information Thompson had given me until I had my face-to-face with Max. "Can you get someone aboard *Duchess* today? Without being seen?"

He laughed. "I'll run it as an exercise. The boys'll love it."

"Thompson may have somebody watching the marina."

"Whatever. They'll never know. What do you need?"

I told him, giving him the whole list.

"I'll have one of the local boys from Ford Island deliver it. Where are you?"

I told him. "It's a high-security building. You can't get in without keys and electronic security cards."

"You have been out of harness for a long time. Would it stop you?"

"No."

"My boys are young, John, but they're not babies. Even the ones who look like babies can bite. They'll be there with what you need in two hours."

"There's no rush."

"The men have to have a schedule. No stress, no fun. Two hours."

VVVVVVVV

27

M y briefcase arrived one hour and fifty-three minutes later. I knew the exact time because the young man who delivered it handed me a buck slip along with my brief-case. He was seven minutes early.

"Senior Chief White wanted you to sign for it," he told me, proud of his achievement and wanting to show off a little. "He wanted you to know that things haven't gone entirely down-hill since you left."

I was beginning to like the kid.

"Everything there?"

"Cellular telephone, knife, your forty-five, ammunition and your watch and wallet. Everything on my list, sir. Anything else you wanted?"

"You have trouble finding anything?"

"No, sir. I like your *Atlas of Asia.*"

"You got an extra Phrobis handy?"

He reached under his blue Aloha shirt and pulled out the black SEAL knife, a twin of the one Thompson had taken from me. "Here," he said. "You might need it."

I took the little knife and felt the edge of the blade. It could draw blood.

"Thanks," I said. "You have any trouble? Was anyone watching my boat?"

"She's being watched, sir. Two men, maybe three, alternating locations. They're now being watched. We'll see where they go."

"Did Chief White ask you to do that?"

The young man seemed surprised by my question. "No, sir. He didn't. I'm running this as part of the exercise."

I smiled at that. Max would have denied them permission to interfere with the investigation. This young fellow was acting on his own initiative. I understood that. It's always easier to do something and later be told you shouldn't have than to ask permission and be told you can't. This man had a future if he didn't shoot down his own career first.

"Mr. Caine?"

I knew what was coming. He wanted in. I didn't blame him. In his place, at his age and with his training I'd do the same thing.

"I'd like to say, uh, if you need anything, anything at all, uh, here's my pager number." He handed me a slip of paper with a local telephone number scrawled across it.

"This authorized?"

"No, sir. I'd be on my own time."

I looked at him carefully. He was eager and competent, and dangerous. A backup.

"What's your name?"

"Jeff, sir."

"Thank you, Jeff," I said. "I'll hang on to this."

"Twenty-four hours, sir. Me and Doug, that's my partner. We discussed it. Call us anytime. We'll come."

What do you say to that? The offer was genuine, and unlike most offers of assistance this one had weight behind it. "Thank you," I said. "I appreciate that. You never know."

He nodded. "I know."

I understood that to mean exactly what he said. He *knew*.

162

"Good luck, sir."

"Thanks again. I hope I won't need it." I closed the door. He would find his own way out. That wasn't a problem, considering the fire codes. These buildings were designed to keep people from coming in. Getting out was easy. Unauthorized entry of a high-security building was a formidable task, but one that didn't seem to have bothered young Jeff at all.

I took the briefcase to the kitchen table and opened it. My pocket cellular telephone and its charger rested on one side of the case, my Colt .45 was nestled in its pancake holster on the other. Eight magazines surrounded the pistol.

I picked up one of the Devel clips and checked it. It was loaded. Bright brass showed through the view ports at the sides of the magazine. Two additional boxes of cartridges were stored on the bottom of the briefcase where they would not tend to move during transit. My Buckmaster was there with the leather shoulder rig I'd had made for it in Hong Kong. My Rolex and my wallet were also in the case.

I found Kate's gun cleaning kit, spread the morning newspaper over the top of her kitchen table, disassembled the Colt and cleaned and oiled it, piece by piece. I unloaded and disassembled each magazine and cleaned its component parts, too, making sure that each spring was in proper position and had the proper tension. I oiled and greased the slide of the Colt and assembled the big pistol again. Then I carefully loaded each of the magazines. When I was finished I loaded one of the eight-round magazines into the butt of the automatic.

Now I felt whole.

I don't like guns. They are noisy and dangerous and they kill people. They bestow a deadly power on people who, upon reflection, might not have hurt anyone seriously if the means weren't so handy, or on people who are too emotionally unstable to handle any kind of power in the first place. They are far too easy to use and require no training to be lethal.

Emotionally I tend to agree with the antigun lobby that peo-

163

ple should not be allowed to possess them. I also don't like the idea of governments having nuclear weapons. Any government. But both the guns and the bomb are realities, have been since before my birth. Once those genies were out of the bottle there is no way to put them back inside. Technology is a wonderful thing but it is also risky. Once a weapon is loosed upon society it stays out there until it is replaced by something even more fearsome. Reality, like truth, can't be outlawed, can't be called back, and can never be stamped out simply because it presents an unpleasantness. If the opposition was armed—and I had a throbbing reminder high up on the back of my leg that the opposition was not only armed, but armed with automatic weapons—I'd be crazy to consider going up against them with anything less than my own firepower. I trusted the Colt. Like me, it had history.

I had my personal arsenal spread out in front of me and was honing my Buckmaster when Kate came home. She looked from the Colt to the big knife, surprise showing on her face in spite of her attempt to hide it.

"You went out." It was a statement that bordered on accusation. She'd been planning on kissing me, or hugging me, but there was no intimacy now. The fact of the weapons had created an invisible wall.

"It was delivered," I said, continuing to sharpen the blade.

"Somebody I know?"

"Probably not."

She crossed her arms in front of her chest and looked at me as she digested that piece of news.

"Thompson's boat is being repaired," she said. "One of his thugs went down to the boat yard this morning and paid to have *Pele* hauled and repaired. Apparently there is some sort of a rush on the order. I've been told a premium was paid to get the work done quickly. You should be proud of yourself. From what I heard you cost him a small fortune."

"Any sign of him?"

"He hasn't been seen at his office and if he is in the house in Haleiwa he didn't show himself all day. We've got close surveillance on both the boat and the house." She shook her hair out of her eyes, wiping her forehead with one slender hand. She seemed unhappy and preoccupied.

"We got a positive ID on one of the men you fought with downtown at Honolulu Hale the other day. His name's William Stone, aka Stony. Originally from New York where he collected seven misdemeanors, drifted out to California where he did the weight club circuit and worked as a bouncer and sometime enforcer. He got into trouble three years ago in San Francisco. Aggravated assault. Served six months of an eighteen-month sentence, then dropped out of sight. He was wanted for parole violation and for questioning about some felony strong-arm robberies in Los Angeles.

"You put him in the hospital with a broken spleen and damaged kidneys. He had an emergency operation at Queens the day after your fight."

"He's low budget and not very smart. And he's in a tight spot," I said. "He'll talk to you."

She pursed her lips, concentrating.

"He was willing to," she said.

"Was? What changed his mind?"

"He knew about some of the things Thompson was into. We offered to ease up on him a little after sentencing. You know, put in a good word with the judge to give him a little less stiff sentence?"

"Not a plea bargain?"

"We don't do that when we've got them by the balls. He was a parole violator, not a defendant. The feds filed on him for interstate flight. He was going back inside. Anyway, he'd agreed to give us a short statement. Somebody got to him first."

"Dead?"

"In the hospital. The night nurse found him last night, throat cut ear to ear."

"You didn't have a guard on him?"

She shook her head. "Guy got a phone call. Went down the hall for two minutes. The nurse found Stone before the guard got back. A quick in and out. Very professional."

"Wow," I said. From what I had seen of Thompson's people, none of them were of that caliber. They were thugs, getting along by being bullies. They might shoot you in the back but they would not cut your throat. That took a special kind of toughness I hadn't seen in them.

"I know. The captain's hot. And you have an alibi. If I were not absolutely certain of your whereabouts last night I'd be suspicious."

I laughed, but then realized she was serious. She was looking at the Phrobis knife on the table and the big one in my hand.

"Thompson plays rough, doesn't he?"

"Yeah."

"But you can't prove it's connected to him."

Her beeper went off. She looked at the display and frowned. "The boss," she said. She went to the kitchen phone and made the call. The conversation was short and I got the impression it was not friendly. But something had happened. I could almost see the hair on the back of her neck rise. She hung up and looked at me.

"*Pele*'s going back in the water this evening. The yard got the call from Thompson and they called us. We can make it if we hurry."

"Thompson's going to be there?"

"We don't know, but we don't think so. His crew is picking up the boat and taking it out. The captain thinks that Thompson is going to meet the boat somewhere."

I started packing my weapons into the briefcase.

"What are you doing?"

"Getting my gear."

"You're not going anywhere with that stuff. You're staying out of this."

"Then why am I going?"

She shook her head. "Because I don't trust you alone. Pack up your stuff and stow it here. Get dressed. You're going with me. I don't want to have to arrest you tonight."

VVVVVVVV

28

Kate drove and I was grateful. I also was grateful to be out of her apartment. People speak of rock fever, the fear of being trapped on a tiny island in the middle of the Pacific. I'd been trapped in a small apartment on a tiny island in the middle of the Pacific for two days and I was beginning to go stir-crazy.

The boat yard was west of downtown in the industrial district of Kaka'ako and traffic was heavy all the way from Waikiki. It was rush hour. Distances are close in Honolulu, but there are many impediments to traveling in a car on an island where there are more vehicles than people. The crush of automobiles was compounded by street closures, barricades and traffic cones, proving the old saying that in Honolulu the shortest distance between two points is always under construction.

By the time we arrived on the western side of Kewalo Boat Harbor the sun was going down. Silhouettes of party boats glided across a mandarin orange horizon. Explosions of white light sparkled across the party craft like strobe lights as tourists memorialized the event.

Kate parked the Mustang and we walked together to the warehouse offices. There was a void in the previous intimacy that I understood as the rebuilding of her armor. My weapon preparation, which she had inadvertently witnessed, had affronted her sense of justice. It was an abrogation of some undefined pact we had made that we were out to get Thompson arrested. If there was some kind of pact I had not been aware of it. My mission was to get the evidence first, and then place Thompson in a position where MacGruder's daughter would not be an issue. If he went to trial, she was certain to become an issue. I could not risk that in order to see him tried in a court of law.

As we climbed the exterior stairway of the warehouse I noticed *Pele* alongside the repair dock across the water. Workmen were finishing their tasks, hurrying before the sun completed its own daily travel. The repairs to *Pele* must have been inconsequential to have been completed in one day. I felt disappointed. Next time I got the chance I would hurt Thompson a little more.

Once inside we joined a small group of men and women who were intent on the big white yacht across the harbor. I recognized Captain Yoshida, and I thought I saw a couple of familiar HPD detectives, but most of the others were unknown to me. They had that confident look of law enforcement types who could not be fired regardless of how badly they screwed up. I assumed them to be feds.

Yoshida was standing in the middle of a group of people, all wearing identical expressions of self-importance. He glanced in our direction as we entered and frowned when he saw me. He waved Kate over, making a small production of ignoring my presence.

I strolled over to a window and watched the activity on *Pele* and the sudden realization of the scope of my failure hit me with the force of a tidal wave. My mission was to destroy any evidence that could implicate MacGruder's daughter and I had led a federal task force to the source. With all this official interest my mission had foundered.

I had hoped to dart into the open jaws of the situation, re-

cover and destroy whatever evidence there was, and then nim-
bly leap out before the jaws snapped shut. That was the plan,
but I found I wasn't nimble enough. There was too much heat
now. The official minions of the law would take it from here,
seizing Thompson, his thugs, his boat, his houses and all his
tapes, rendering my cause hopeless.

I didn't like failure. What was worse was the possibility of
seeing a good man lose his career for something his daughter
had done.

Across the water two men boarded *Pele*. Something was exchanged with one of the workmen, who left the boat, lugging
tools and electrical cords. One of the two men went below
while the other went to the flying bridge. A puff of blue smoke
discharged from the exhaust and the water below the stern
roiled from the spinning propellers.

Twenty hands brought twenty cellular phones and radio
sets to twenty mouths at nearly the same instant. If stares really did have weight *Pele* would have sunk then and there. The
big yacht moved away from the dock, making for the breakwater and the open ocean through a bright, tropical sunset.

It was over, I thought. Thompson was out there somewhere, expecting his men to pick him up and take him to the
next port. With the craft properly provisioned, Thompson could
make the mainland or he could make Tahiti.

But *Pele* was not properly provisioned. Kate's contact at the
boat yard had reported only minor repairs. She had not mentioned provisioning. And none of that mattered anyhow, because the feds would swoop down and pick them up before
they entered international waters. And a thought hit me.

Thompson was merely evil. He wasn't stupid and he wasn't
a fool. With someone like me nosing around, he must have
known that something was going to happen, and that serious
heat would soon follow. *Pele* was the bait, a queen's gambit, the
magnet that would draw all of the official attention. On this
planet there is nothing more controlled, taxed, licensed, in-

spected and surveyed than an ocean-going vessel. A big yacht is slow, and on the ocean it presents a target profile similar to one of those stationary Iraqi tanks that were annihilated during the Gulf War. If Thompson expected any kind of official interest, *Pele* would be the last place he would be found.

I looked for Kate. She was in deep conversation with her boss, her face a study in beauty and passion in motion. It was not a good time to interrupt.

I watched and waited. Kate left her group and stood next to me by the window.

"They hit his house in Haleiwa this afternoon," she told me. "No one was there but they found tire tracks that might match those found at the MacGruder scene. It looked as though Thompson had packed and left the house in a hurry."

"They expect him to be aboard *Pele?*"

"They expect he'll meet the yacht once it's left port."

I nodded. They would expect that. But he wouldn't be there.

"Thompson has no chance of getting off this island," Kate continued. "The airport is blanketed. Are you all right?" Her dark eyes were shining, the passion there reminiscent of the night before. This woman was a warrior, in her own element, closing in for the kill.

"I'm fine," I said. "I just thought it would turn out differently."

"You're still worried about those tapes."

I nodded.

"This will ruin MacGruder."

I nodded again.

"And you don't want that to happen."

"No, Kate, I don't."

"It has to be this way. You understand that, don't you?"

I shook my head. "I understand that you think it has to be this way."

This time Kate nodded, impatiently, biting her lower lip. She was looking at this from her own perspective. There wasn't room for another. "I've got to get back to the others. I made a mistake bringing you here, I can see that now. I just didn't want you to get in the way. There are some heavy people out there looking for Thompson and you could get caught in the cross-fire."

"I'll get by," I said.

"That wasn't what I meant! You get in the way and there's no way I can help you. You'll be looking at serious felony charges if you obstruct this investigation in any way. They know why you're here! I explained that to my boss, that I brought you here to keep you out of the way. He didn't buy all of it, but you've got to help yourself now. I can't help you any-more!"

She returned to the official group of Thompson-hunters without another word, her back held tense and absolutely straight by the depth of her feelings. I'd seen that before, recognized it from previous desertions. I had become excess baggage. She was angry with me for not accepting this as the proper and logical conclusion of the chase. If things turned out my way there would be a miscarriage of justice.

There's more than one kind of justice.

While the full force and might of the City and County of Honolulu, the state of Hawaii and the United States of America prepared to descend upon the hapless crew of *Pele*, I slipped from the warehouse. I knew I wouldn't be missed. I also knew where I could go to get a lead on where Thompson might be found.

I made my way through the dying tropical summer day to a waiting taxi stand and climbed into the back seat of the first one I found. I gave the driver the address of the old Young Street police station. I had the keys Kate had given me and I would need my Jeep to find Thompson.

My wounds were healing and I was rested and ready. It was time to come out of hiding and try to salvage this thing if I could.

VVVVVVV

29

No one stopped me when I walked to the middle of the impound yard at the old police station, peeled the pink impound sign from the windshield of my Jeep and drove off. I didn't even consider my next step. There wasn't another choice.

I parked in the tow away zone in front of the restaurant. I didn't think the Jeep would get towed again. Not in front of Chawlie's place. It was early for his usual appearance but I knew he'd show up as soon as one of his people called him. The hit order on me would be no secret in Chinatown and I wondered just how fast the news of my invasion of his headquarters would carry back to him. There would be a reward attached and I didn't think it would take long.

A waiter reluctantly took my order, probably worried I wouldn't live long enough to tip him. The kitchen was unusually slow delivering the food and when it came Chawlie still hadn't arrived. I sat with my back toward the restaurant's entrance to demonstrate my disdain for the threat to my life. It was my way of gaining face while simultaneously insulting Chawlie. I wasn't afraid of offending him. He'd already threatened to kill me. I ate my hot and sour soup, hoping it wasn't poisoned.

When I finished the soup I asked for my bill. The waiter smiled, went to the front desk and came back with a plastic tray that was empty except for a single fortune cookie.

"Boss say no charge for you, Mr. Caine."

The waiter bowed and backed away from my table. I took the fortune cookie and opened it and read the note. It said, A GREAT FORTUNE IS IN YOUR FUTURE. I had expected a cryptic message like, KISS YOUR ASS GOODBYE, ROUND EYE! but that was apparently beyond even Chawlie's capabilities. Threats in a fortune cookie were a little too subtle even for him.

No one approached my table with verbal cryptic messages, either, the way they used to in the old movies where the mysterious Oriental delivers the warning out of the side of his mouth. My own waiter didn't return. I finished the rest of the pot of tea and waited. I'd been there forty-five minutes, long enough for Chawlie to arrive, but he wasn't showing and I wondered again if I'd made a mistake.

I got up and threw a couple of bills on the table. The waiter smiled at me the way you'd smile at a person who was dying of cancer—warm, meaningful, ghastly. I smiled back, hoping to scare him. I left the restaurant and nearly ran Chawlie over, stumbling before I walked into his chair in the foyer. There was another orange plastic chair across from him and he motioned for me to sit.

"You let Australian devil shoot you. I told you, too many people shoot you."

"Good afternoon, Chawlie."

"You stupid, or what?"

"I need your help."

"Help? Help you? Not you. My son is dead because of you."

"You set him up! For the honor of the family!"

He looked at me, blueberry eyes alive with emotion, but trying desperately not to expose the passion there. "I told you I'd kill you if you come here again, John Caine."

174

"You said a lot of things, Chawlie. Most of which was total crap."

"You did not believe me?"

"Of course not. You need me and I need you. My job is to destroy Thompson and his evidence. You just want him destroyed. He ruined your son even before he killed him. You used a little spy to infiltrate his company. She got tossed to the sharks. You used your son, you used me and you used her, too! Don't deny it. Now Thompson knows everything your son knew and everything Jasmine knew, too. Thompson's a torture freak. They would not have lied."

Chawlie said nothing. He didn't change expression during my speech. He just sat there and listened and aged twenty years.

"You can't deny it. Thompson told me all about it just before he killed me. Or tried to."

"It is difficult to kill you."

"Don't you ever forget that, Chawlie."

Chawlie stared at me, betraying nothing. He had conquered the emotions boiling within him. I waited, knowing he was considering his options and trying to pick his best one. I already knew what it was but I wanted him to find it on his own.

"You are not afraid to die."

He was beginning the negotiations with the hard sell. If that was his opener he had already lost.

"Not me. But anyone you send better be ready."

Chawlie nodded. "What do you want?"

"The police have already raided his properties and offices and come up empty. Thompson must have another home here, somewhere the cops don't know about. He's someplace on this rock and he probably owns the property and it's probably under the name of a cutout or a shell corporation he controls. You know it. You know where it is. You've known it since the day he bought the place. You know everything that goes on here that affects you. I need that address and I need it now."

Chawlie shook his head. "It is very difficult—"

"Cut the crap, Chawlie! You know where it is! Don't lie to me!"

"I'm not sure there is another—"

"Look. You owe me. If not for what you did to me, then for what I did for you. And if that's not good enough, then for what Jasmine did for you! And for what you did to your son! You want to destroy Thompson? I'm your man. No charge. Just give me the address! Now!"

"Property under the name of a Nevada corporation, officers all foreign nationals. Devil Thompson thinks no one can find out. I know before he put the check in the bank. Broker my nephew, bank president my cousin." Chawlie gave me the location of the only other piece of property Thompson owned on the island. It was on a ridge above Haleiwa, surrounded by cane fields.

"Anyone else know this?"

"Only me. Now you." Chawlie would not look me in the eye. This had cost him a lot of face. "What are you going to do?"

"Take him out. Any way I can."

Chawlie looked at me. The passion was coming back. "You got cause."

"Yeah," I reminded him. "And so do you."

I got up to leave, keys in my hand.

"John Caine!"

I stopped and turned back toward Chawlie. He had not moved from his chair but his head was turned toward me, his mouth open as if he were struggling with himself. I don't know which side won. "My nephew, a contractor, built a basement under this house. Be careful. He has secret entrance to basement from house. You would not find it if you didn't know it was there."

"You're sure?"

"Yes. Sure. He make his movies there. People scream and no one hear them."

"Where is it?"

"Don't know. You could ask nephew, but he's on vacation. You look. You'll find it. Small house."

"Thank you, Chawlie. It helps."

"You don't have to worry about having to die anymore, John Caine. I no kill you now. Thompson do it, I think."

In the reflection of the neon lights in the windows of the shops along River Street I watched the old man watching me as I got into my Jeep and drove away.

YYYYYYY

30

The ocean's surface retained a clear delineation with the sky six hours after the sun had slipped below the horizon. Light from a full moon reflected off the waves, painting their tops with silver all the way to the edge of the world.

I lay on my stomach in a stand of mature sugar cane trying to impose myself into the terrain, ignoring the possibility of centipedes and scorpions that inhabited these fields like commuters on the L.A. freeways. The cane was dry and ready for harvest and it made a hissing sound when the breezes blew in from off the sea.

From Chawlie's restaurant I had driven directly to my berth in Pearl Harbor, not bothering to scout the area before boarding *Duchess*, wondering, but not caring, if Thompson's people were watching me, and if SEALs were watching them.

My briefcase was still in Kate's apartment, so I retrieved more weapons and changed to black fatigues and jump boots. I drove directly to Haleiwa, through the rolling pineapple and sugar cane that covered the central plains of Oahu. Nobody followed me. The freeway ran all the way from Waipahu to Wahiawa, terminating at Schofield Barracks. From there it branched into a couple of two-lane country roads. Only one of the narrow little cane roads led from Wahiawa to Haleiwa. No one could follow me without exposing their presence. It was too flat and too narrow, especially in the dark.

The map book of Oahu showed the property's address on a dead-end street. I drove by the house anticipating a quiet rural neighborhood, the kind of setting you'd expect in an affluent environment. I was surprised. The house was the only one on the street, its concrete driveway the only one that did not lead to a grass plot. Two police cruisers flanked the house and two more were parked in the street. Chawlie wasn't the only one with connections.

Seven people conferred in a group in the front yard. Huddled together, they had a collective end-of-shift attitude, as if nothing of importance had occurred. Their postures were those of hunters who had missed the game, fishermen without a bite. Their faces, hidden behind sunglasses, tracked me in the Jeep as I drove past. I stared back, an errant tourist.

It was disappointing, but not surprising that the cops beat me to the house. Government agencies can, when they put their collective minds to it, shift monumental piles of paper to find connections so seemingly trivial as to defy logic. That's their strength. But they couldn't know what wasn't written, filed, entered and collated. They didn't know Chawlie. That's their weakness.

The sun was gone and I drove all the way to the end of the road before turning back. This time I ignored them, concentrating on how to get to the cane field behind the house. I noted the position of the house. It was an intruder upon the field, surrounded on three sides by the cane. I wanted to get into position before it became too dark and too quiet.

If Chawlie's information was correct I wanted to get inside the house and look around. When I made the slow reconnaissance I noted large windows all the way around the house, a standard Hawaiian architectural device for maximum ventilation. From the exterior of the structure, nothing seemed to match the layout of the room where I suspected the tapes were made. The secret basement that Chawlie had mentioned must certainly be there. The house looked to be slab on grade, but that didn't mean anything. The basement didn't have to be directly ventilated to the outside. Bomb shelters don't have windows.

Thompson could be hiding there until the search for him cooled off. Even the feds don't have the funds or the energy to continue a high-profile manhunt for long. After a few days they would conclude he had left the island and would depend upon other means to catch him.

Thompson would have had a back door in place long ago. A man in his position would have known it wouldn't last, no matter how self-delusionary he was in other respects. It was a gamble, but the police and the feds had covered all the other exists. They'd pierced the tangled corporate vines Thompson used to conceal his ownership of the property, and it followed they would know everything else about him, too.

He had to be somewhere and I had nowhere else to go. If Thompson was on the island, he would be hiding in that basement.

The cops were gone by the time I got into place at the edge of the cane. They had left a solitary vehicle parked in the driveway with a lone occupant. He appeared to be listening to the radio and drinking a cup of coffee, waiting out the time until his replacement arrived. He clearly expected no trouble.

As I lay in the cane watching the cop my thoughts returned to Kate's frustration at my actions. She must have felt betrayed. I hadn't promised her I wouldn't pursue my own mission. Somehow she had assumed that just because we'd become lovers we were allies, that her goals and desires were now mine. I owed a debt to MacGruder, and as long as it was still possible to repay it my goals wouldn't change.

Headlights appeared from the direction of the highway. A car stopped in the driveway, beside the cop's car. I strained to hear the conversation but there was a steady breeze whispering through the cane and I could hear nothing else. From their relaxed postures it appeared they were two men who knew each other well. A third person occupied the shotgun seat, and for an instant I caught the profile of a woman. The driver lit a cigarette and the lighter briefly illuminated Kate's face. Had the interception of *Pele* gone so wrong that now Kate was out beating the bushes again?

Another vehicle came down the road, a dark cargo van with no windows in the rear compartment. Kate and the other two cops swiveled their heads toward the van. Beyond the two police cars, just in the periphery of my vision, I saw a door open and a shadow detach itself from the house.

The van stopped at the end of the drive, blocking the two police cars, and sat idling its engine, getting the full attention of the occupants of the police cars.

I tried to get my gun out of its holster below my fatigue blouse, but the breeze suddenly waned and every movement I made caused the dry cane around me to rattle. I rolled to one side and put my hand under my left arm and tried to draw the big revolver. I saw the interior lights of one car flash on as the uniformed cop got out of his car to investigate.

Two muffled shots came from the house and the cop dropped to the ground. Two more shots were fired into the driver's side of the windshield of the other police car. Then two more.

I lay frozen in place, on my right side, right arm under my fatigue blouse, hand on my Ruger Redhawk .44 magnum. Another breeze wandered through the cane field. I took advantage of the noise and drew the revolver.

The shadow emerged from the darkness and stood over the body of the policeman lying between the two cars. The man was a big Asian I had not seen before, big as a sumo wrestler. He fired again, aiming toward the body at his feet. He kicked at the body, grunted, and opened the driver's door of the nearest car, his pistol extended.

A small figure darted from the passenger door and raced for

the street. I recognized her at once. Head down, arms pumping, feet flying over the driveway, Kate looked like she had a chance to escape until the back door of the van opened and two men jumped out and tackled her to the concrete. One of the men hit her with his fist after she went down.

The big man pulled the other body from the car. It was Captain Yoshida, Kate's boss. The big Asian dragged Yoshida and the other dead policeman into the house. At the van the two men turned Kate over and searched her roughly, and after a short conference, hauled her into the van and closed the cargo doors.

There was an opening in the hurricane fence surrounding the property that looked wide enough to drive through. If there had been a road at one time it was long gone, reclaimed by the vegetation. The sumo wrestler came out of the house and drove each police car into the cane until they were no longer visible. He piled cut cane around the last car until he was satisfied they were covered and returned to the house.

The van's occupants remained hidden. I didn't know Kate's condition, but her captivity changed the equation. I couldn't rush them now. Waiting was all I could do.

Thompson came out of the house preceded by the big Asian and followed by Tweedledee. Each man carried two satchels.

I tracked the big Asian with my Ruger, judging him to be the most dangerous. When I had a shot I fired a double-hammer, two shots into the man's chest. As he went down I moved my sights and shot Tweedledee twice. I emptied the gun toward where I thought Thompson had been. By then everybody was down and I was moving, retreating into the cane field, rolling, crabbing sideways, back and away from the light, ejecting the empty shells and searching for a speedloader as I moved.

I'd counted Thompson plus four men, including the two in the van. I'd taken out two with my assault. That left two plus Thompson. I didn't really count him. He wasn't the type to run around a dark cane field searching for an armed man. I could see him ordering someone else to do it but I couldn't see him going himself.

I crawled to a rough row of old tire tracks gouged into the soil and covered by cane. I'd scouted the field on the way in, choosing this as my first fallback position. I waited, knowing they'd come.

They did. Four of them, flanking me in two lines.

Four?

I lay motionless, allowing them to pass me in the dense cane. When the last man passed I eased myself onto my elbows and shot him in the back. He bellowed in pain and pitched forward, throwing what looked like an automatic weapon into the darkness in front of him. I fired on where I thought the drag man would be on the other line. Then I ran.

Automatic weapons fire opened up behind me. I dropped to the ground and rolled to my right. An invisible harvester cut the tops of the sugar cane above my head. I lay on the ground, hugging the tire tracks, and reloaded.

The only advantage I had was invisibility. They didn't know my location unless I fired on them or moved. That went both ways but they had to move and time was running out. They outnumbered me, but someone somewhere would have heard the shots and called the police. I'd hit three, so there should only be two left, but I was hearing four, one moaning complaints but still upright.

It wasn't possible. A .44 magnum will put a man down and keep him there. Hit a man with one and he wouldn't be able to get up and complain about his injuries unless he was wearing a bulletproof vest.

That possibility had not occurred to me. I had no armor-piercing ammunition. I'd been firing stepped-down magnums, as accurate and easy to control as hot-loaded .44 Specials. I hadn't figured on Kevlar. I did have maximum-loaded magnum ammunition capable of knocking down a grizzly, the same load I'd used on the shark. It might not penetrate the Kevlar, but it would give them something to think about. I dumped the rounds from the cylinder and replaced them with max loads.

From a position deep in the cane I lay immobile, waiting for them to make the next move. The wind shifted, blowing steadily from off the ocean, obscuring the softer noises. Thompson's men were quiet, hunkered down, waiting for me to do something. They had learned a great deal over the past few minutes. Any time they moved I shot them. Even with body armor it couldn't have been fun. A Kevlar vest provides protection against fatal injuries, spreading the shock throughout the garment's fibers, but it is still like getting hit with a baseball bat, and the .44 was at the upper end of the protection capabilities of most vests.

The breeze became stronger, rattling the cane around me and masking any movements. It heightened my senses. Had I been in their position I would have used the distraction of the wind to charge.

They came head on, firing as they went. Bullets zinged by me, cutting stalks and plowing into the dirt. One of the men came raging out of the cane ten feet away and I aimed carefully and shot him in the upper thigh. He fell forward and I shot him through the top of the head. Both shots were accompanied by a three-foot cone of orange flame from the end of the Ruger's barrel.

I rolled toward my left as the night exploded. The others saturated the area where I had been, filling the empty space with bullets.

A muzzle flash was visible through the stalks and I returned fire, hoping to hit something not covered by armor. My shot lit up the night. The muzzle flash stopped. Two other guns were directed my way and I jumped sideways, rolling to safer ground.

I snapped off a shot toward the nearest weapon, knowing it was a miss. Then the night went quiet.

Thompson's unmistakable voice ordered his men from the

cane. From the sounds around me, three men were making every effort to obey as quickly as they could. I held my fire.

"Thompson!" I shouted into the black night. "I'm coming after you!"

There was a silence, almost a tangible shock wave running through the cane. Mine was probably the last voice he would have expected to hear.

"Not bloody likely, Caine!"

"You can't kill me, Thompson!"

"I've got a hostage. You come any closer I'll pop the little policewoman, and it'll be your fault!"

Kate was still alive. How much longer, and how she would spend her remaining hours was not something I wanted to think about. I only wanted her free. I took inventory and assessed my situation. I'd brought enough ammunition to celebrate a Chinese New Year, but I could not bring an attack on them through the cane. Physically I was hurting and weak. The pain was tolerable, the adrenaline helping to cover most of it, but my injuries slowed me down.

The tapes had to be with Thompson. They were far too valuable to be out of his sight. But their recovery was far outweighed by Kate. She was alive and breathing, and I had to get her away from him before getting to the tapes.

I didn't think Thompson would run until he was certain I was dead, and he wouldn't count on that until he saw the body this time. I began crawling quietly toward the house, the massive revolver in front of me.

The breeze intensified, blowing in off the water. It brought with it a new smell. The smell of fire.

I saw the glow of flames moving toward me, fueled by the night breezes behind it. Thompson had called his men from the cane to set it on fire. He was going to burn me out.

I ran.

I tried to take a perpendicular track to the flames but they were on a broad front. I didn't gain anything with that maneuver, I only lost ground. I changed directions and ran for my life.

Halfway across the field was a small stream, nearly five feet across and several feet deep. It was supposed to be my second fallback position. The fire was moving fast and I hoped to beat the wall of flame to the stream. Making the far edge of the field was impossible, but I might make it halfway.

I ran for another thirty seconds and realized even the stream was too far. The cane was too dense to run through and the flames were licking at my heels. My injuries were also catching up with me. Even with the terror of the flames I just didn't have the energy I needed.

I ran at an angle to the flames, searching for an opening. There was only one chance left. If I could find a spot where the fire was sparse I could risk jumping back through, landing on the other side. If it was moving fast enough, and if there was another side and not just more fire. That wasn't the best option, but it was the only one left.

And then I didn't even have that option. The fire swept up and boiled over me like a white-hot orange wave. I sprinted straight into the flames as fast as I could run.

VVVVVVVV

31

As the fire reached me I leapt into the air as if I could hurdle the wall of flame. I obeyed my instincts. Having no operational experience in anything like this, I held my breath and closed my eyes, covering them with my hands.

The heat and smoke seemed to be worse before I jumped than while I was inside the flames. There was no conscious realization other than a buffeting of warm winds that seemed to come from hell itself, tendrils wrapping around my legs and tickling the hair behind my ears. I seemed to float above the earth for an eternity, weightless as an ash from a fireplace borne into the sky.

Then I hit the stalks of singed cane on the other side of the fire and the hard-packed earth below. My heels hit first and I rolled forward in a perfect paratrooper landing. I continued the roll until I was standing again and the flames burned behind me, turning the cane into barren stalks.

My clothes were smoldering but the hard-surfaced cotton had not burned and I didn't seem much worse off than before. Warm viscous fluid leaked down the back of my leg from the reopened bullet wound. The hair on the backs of my hands was black and stubbed, and I guessed that the hair on my head would look much the same. My face felt as if I'd been out in

187

the sun too long, but I could see and I could walk with not much more appreciable pain than before.

"I am alive," I said.

I checked the loads in the Ruger and began jogging through the stubbled cane toward the house. It didn't take long. I hadn't run as far as I thought before the fire overtook me. The two police cars were still in the unburned cane, out of the path of the fire storm. The flames would get to them only if the winds shifted.

I found the body of the man I'd shot. The fire had not been kind.

At the fence I found an opening in the chain link, the one Thompson's man had used. The van was gone, the house and grounds dark. I tried the door to the house and found it unlocked.

I took a flashlight from my pack and entered the dark structure, the light in my left hand, the .44 in my right.

It was an unremarkable house, unpretentious and sparsely furnished. It was not what I would have expected from Thompson, but it would have been an excellent cover for the snuff film production house.

The bodies of Yoshida and the other policeman were sprawled on the floor of the kitchen, blood congealing under them in a black syrupy pool. Both men had been shot in the head. From the amount of blood it looked as though their hearts had continued to beat for a while after the trauma.

Possibly the only reason the police had not found the entrance to the cellar was because they had not been looking for one. If they knew what I knew they would have torn the structure down and jackhammered the slab. I had some rudimentary knowledge of how these things were constructed. I looked in closets.

A trapdoor can be concealed wall to wall in a small area. It cannot be hidden in a large room. I found it on my third try. The master bedroom had two closets. One had nothing but shoe racks, lining each wall, floor to ceiling. The other had hanging clothing. I took a long look and decided the shoes.

The shoe racks started at the floor, making the actual floor area that much smaller, about three feet by five feet, a good size for a trapdoor that had to accommodate material and equipment. And dead bodies. I searched the perimeter of the racks and found the latch, hidden just under the carpet.

I pushed the latch and lifted the trapdoor until it locked in place. I descended wooden stairs, my flashlight held before me like a magic wand to ward off evil spirits. I put my revolver away. Whatever was down here would not be afraid of a gun.

When I reached a landing I found I could stand without hitting my head and closed the hatch behind me. This is North Shore Oahu, and police and fire equipment are far away. The police would want to contact their own people on the site first. Unless someone reported hearing the shots they would become alarmed only when they couldn't raise them. The closest units were either Wahiawa or Kuhuku, each about twenty minutes distant. The fire department was closer, but they would come out, find a cane field burning, contact the sugar company and stand by to see that the fire didn't get out of control.

I tried a switch and a light came on.

The studio occupied one half of the room. The torture rack was partially disassembled, its parts leaning against the wall. Forensics should be able to match splinters taken from Mary MacGruder's body with pieces of that rack. The paneling looked familiar. The carpet was similar. I wondered how many innocents had died in this dim little room.

Three depressions were worn in the carpet where a heavy tripod had stood. I squatted behind the triangle to sight the room and saw that the camera angle was identical to that in the two tapes Thompson had displayed. Looking to my left, I visualized the place where the two men had stood with the girl before they butchered her. I stared at the spot and could almost feel her terror.

A wall of tapes, floor to ceiling, stood behind me. A snuff library. The cassettes were labeled by number, an obvious code system. There were no clues how to decipher the code. There was no way to be certain I could get any of Mary's tapes, much less all of them. I had the feeling that Thompson took most of the Mary tapes as well as a representative sample of the others, as many as he could carry. He had a day to pick and choose, already knowing the code.

I went upstairs and looked around again. No one had come to the house yet. Flashing lights and activity bustled on the far side of the cane field but no one had yet discovered the house and the cars. The flames had not spread and looked to be dying.

I dragged the bodies of Yoshida and the other murdered policeman from the kitchen and laid them in the driveway, away from the house. The effort winded me and I had to rest at the door, leaning against the jamb. After a few minutes I went back to the basement.

The disassembled cross was even more difficult to move from the basement to the driveway, but I managed to muscle it up the stairs and place the pieces next to the bodies so the wood would be perceived as being significant. I returned to the basement, thinking over my last decision.

If Mary had been murdered over three months before, she would not be in the most recent tapes. There were no dates on the labels, but the ink looked fresher on some than on others. I chose five of what looked to be the newest cassettes and stuffed those in my pack.

I found a can of spray deodorant in the bathroom, took my lighter and held it at arm's length, and sprayed the tiny flamethrower toward the tape library. The plastic cases and the rough pine shelving instantly caught fire. I repeated the process near the floor. When the library was totally involved and I was certain that none of the tapes would survive I left the basement.

I was concerned the air might not draw down to the basement and the flames would smother, so I left the trapdoor open. I opened a couple of windows, too, and left the kitchen door open to give the fire plenty of oxygen. It didn't matter if the house burned completely. I wanted to eliminate all evidence of Mary MacGruder from this place.

After thoroughly wiping down the cassettes, I dropped the five tapes on the bodies of the policemen. I had done all I could for them. With two police cars, one with bullet holes in the windshield, the tapes and the pieces of the rack, the police should be able to put two and two together and come up with at least four.

I walked through unblackened sugar cane toward the spot where I'd hidden my Jeep. It was over a mile away, in the opposite direction of the path of the fire. Once I was out of the light I began jogging. I set an easy pace, one that went well with my injuries and yet would get me to my Jeep in less than ten minutes. I planned to be home in forty minutes after that.

I had to report Kate's abduction, even though that would put me at the fire and the destruction of evidence and three dead bodies, two of whom were policemen. There would be hell to pay, and if the cops could not go after those who did it, they'd destroy anyone still standing. That was me.

I'd started way behind the power curve on this one, and I'd doggedly stayed there. The only thing I could say about my performance so far was that I'd hung in there. Persistence may be a virtue, but it was the only one I'd demonstrated. The rest of my work sure wasn't brilliant.

I'd go after Thompson myself, but I had no idea where he was. I counted on the evidence I left at the scene to heat the police to a fever pitch to find him and rescue Kate. This is a small island, and there are many, many men and women in blue. Thompson would have to leave if he intended to survive.

Hawaii is unique in all the world. It is the most isolated land mass on the planet. In order to leave here it takes a large ocean-going vessel or a capable, long-range airplane. No one leaves in a small private plane. No one can drive away. No one can hitchhike. Everyplace else is too far away.

An idea popped into my mind. Thompson had sacrificed *Pele*. The airport was out of the question. How else was he going to leave? A small boat could rendezvous with a ship. A smaller boat would not be shown on most radar sets. A boat such as a sailboat might even be considered a mote on the screen of all but the most sophisticated military strike radar.

Come on, man, think! The closest marina was down in Haleiwa. If Thompson had gone to so much trouble to hide, he'd also have an alternative way out of the islands. His actions tonight were those of a man with no intention of remaining in Hawaii.

I started running harder. The faster I could get to my Jeep, the faster I'd make the Haleiwa harbor.

VVVVVVV

32

I desperately sought a telephone. I was used to having a cellular, and finding a pay phone was a skill I'd lost. After what
seemed like an endless search I found a working phone at the
back of a restaurant in Haleiwa and reported the shootings and
Kate's kidnapping to a young female 911 dispatcher. I told her
to contact the coast guard, but she ignored my suggestion. She
demanded my name, and when I wouldn't give it to her became officious and abusive. Knowing our conversation was
being taped, and knowing my location appeared on her monitor, I gave her the address of the house in Haleiwa, repeated
the suggestion that the coasties get involved, and hung up.

Haleiwa Boat Harbor was deserted. The ocean was spastic
beyond the breakwater. Erratic waves pitched over the rock
barrier, spilling into the calmer waters inside. A storm lurked
beyond the horizon. Of what size or intensity I couldn't tell, but
there was the heavy, tangible feeling of something huge and
malevolent out there. It was not a night to be out in a small
boat.

I jogged to the end of the dock where two local men were
fishing. They sat on the edge, legs dangling in the water, pole
gripped tightly in one hand, a beer in the other. A Playmate

cooler perched on the deck between them and empty bottles lined the dock like sentinels.

"Did any boats leave here tonight?"

They looked at me as if I'd suddenly materialized from a flying saucer. I realized I still had on my ragged fatigues and my weapons were all too apparent.

"Yah," said the older one after a moment of sizing me up. When I got close I saw a family resemblance between them. "I told my son they was crazy to go out tonight. Big blow coming, I think."

"When did they leave?"

"Dunno. Not long. I opened two beers since they left. Maybe twenty minutes."

"Twenty?"

"Ten or fifteen. I dunno. They was plenty guys, and a woman. She didn't want to go. The big man, he carry her aboard after she hit the other man. She hit him wit' her fist. Good smack, right in the chin. Don't blame her she don't wanna go. Gonna be bad tonight." Kate's fight had been vastly entertaining to watch. And neither man had thought to interfere. Their understanding of the situation was only that a man was having problems with his woman.

"What kind of boat?"

"You some kind of cop?" I'd asked too many questions and aroused their natural suspicions of haoles.

"Does that mean you aren't going to tell me?"

"What's your beef?"

"That woman was kidnapped. The guys who did it killed two cops tonight."

For the first time the fishermen paid attention to what I said. The younger one spoke first. "Sailboat. About thirty feet. Couldn't catch the name, but it's a white sailboat with white sails."

"They're out there in a sailboat?"

"Had a small motor and they was using it, but they also was using their mainsail. Buncha clowns."

"Thank you," I said. I ran back down to the quay and found another pay phone outside the Chart House. When I got the Honolulu Police Department I gave the dispatcher the information I'd just received and hung up when she again started questioning my identity. They'd get to me sooner or later, but there was no way I was going to voluntarily take myself out of the action. I ran to my Jeep and pointed it toward Pearl Harbor. It would take half an hour if I hurried, and hurry was the only thing I could do.

No one was aboard *Duchess* and there was no evidence that anyone had been there since I'd left. Even though I knew the young SEAL had been aboard to retrieve my gear, nothing had been disturbed. Max was right about these kids. The new guys were puppies, but they were good. Possibly better than I'd ever been in my prime.

The telephone rang. I ignored it. I went into my cabin and stripped off my fatigues. They were damaged beyond repair, burnt through at the knees and elbows. The plastic tips of my bootlaces were melted. I put the Ruger away in the gun locker and loaded a more appropriate firearm.

I stared at my face in the mirror. A stranger with a red, boiled face and no eyebrows stared back at me. I pushed a finger into my cheek. The spot I touched remained white for a full thirty seconds before it slowly faded. First- and second-degree burns, nothing worse than a bad sunburn. Not as bad as it could have been. Other images floated to the surface of my consciousness, memories of napalm victims. For years after Vietnam I had been unable to eat barbecued ribs.

The telephone rang again. I let it ring six times. Whoever it was was persistent.

I changed into shorts and a sleeveless gray sweatshirt. My pain was constant now, but it was merely background. My face felt raw and hot. Pain radiated down my right leg from my buttock where I'd been shot. The jellyfish welts felt as bad as they looked. But I was alive and I had a mission. I was running on adrenaline and hope.

The telephone rang again. It was still ringing when I went topside to disconnect the utility connections and to prepare to cast off.

Somewhere out there was a small boat carrying Thompson and Kate and the rest of Thompson's men. I had to make the effort to find them. Their twenty-minute head start had grown to an hour, expanding the possible radius of where they might be. There was little chance of finding them. It was a big ocean and, like Thompson's boat, *Duchess* was small and slow. The only way to look for them efficiently would be in a small aircraft. Even then it would be chancy, especially at night. But I didn't have access to an airplane. All I had was *Duchess*.

Someone came down the dock toward my boat. Only one man. From the cadence of his step I could tell that it was an athletic male wearing tennis shoes.

"Permission to come aboard?"

It was Max. He was carrying a small day pack and dressed in his tourist outfit. He looked ready to play volleyball on the beach, although I knew he must have spent at least six of the past hours on an airplane.

"Come aboard," I said. I wedged the four-barreled .357 magnum derringer back into my hip pocket while he climbed the side of the boat and lightly touched down in the cockpit. He made no noise and *Duchess* shifted only slightly as she adjusted for his weight. "Thought you couldn't make it out here."

"Thought you could use some help."

"I'm damned glad to see you," I said. I worked mechanically, stowing lines and cables. As much as I appreciated it, Max's arrival was not going to interrupt my preparations for departure.

"My people told me it got hairy out there tonight," he said.

"I didn't see anybody," I said.

"They saw you. Said you took on four or five guys armed with automatic weapons and you only had an old six-shooter hand cannon. Said you were okay for an old fart."

"Thompson's got a hostage," I said. "A female police detective. God knows what he's going to do with her."

"I know."

"I was just leaving," I said. "I have places to go."

"I tried calling you."

When I made no reply he went on. "You know you need permission from the harbor master to leave Pearl at night."

"I've already got the FBI, the Honolulu Police Department and the state of Hawaii mad at me. I might as well piss off the navy, too."

"Heard you started a hell of a house fire."

"Listen, partner, I've got to try to find a sailboat that left Haleiwa an hour ago. I don't know where he went, or in which direction, but I've got some ideas. I've got one shot at it and I want to make it my best one."

Max reached into the cargo pocket of his day pack and took out a small black plastic box. "This will help." He laid it on the cushion next to the transom and turned a switch. Red LED numbers lit up a small screen.

"What's that?"

"Radio direction finder. Works on a special frequency. Had people following you. They were under strict orders not to interfere, regardless of what happened. If you were killed they were to return to base and not to speak of anything they saw. When you were not killed they followed the man you are interested in to the boat harbor in Haleiwa. Before the boat left they managed to attach a transmitter to the hull. We've been tracking it ever since."

"And?"

"We can't pick up the signal here because it's line-of-sight and the mountains interfere, but the last bearing we had was off the western coast of Oahu. Heading south."

"Right toward me." I swiveled my head toward the Waianae Mountains. Only the lights of Makakilo sprawled along their eastern flanks made them visible. Otherwise they were a blackness against a greater dark. Somewhere beyond their peaks were Thompson and Kate. I pictured a map with a small sailboat moving toward Barber's Point.

"You can catch them."

"How many people on board?"

"Two men and the hostage. The two men had the others carry the gear aboard the sailboat and then they forced them into a van at gunpoint. They were shot inside the van. My people think they used silenced weapons because they didn't hear any gunshots."

That didn't square with what the local fishermen told me, but they were more intent upon what they thought were the antics of a haole domestic dispute. The activity would have suggested that all the people got aboard when they left the harbor, and if the fishermen had not heard the shots they would conclude that everyone they saw was on the boat.

"And they didn't stop them?"

"They didn't have orders to do that. And they figured you wouldn't mind if there were a few less."

"Why would he shoot his own people?"

Max shook his head. "Lower his overhead. He's on the run. Why take more than you need?"

I pondered that. Max had a point. It would be typical of Thompson. He wouldn't think twice about eliminating anyone who was of no further use. And this man was holding Kate as a hostage.

Max pulled a navigational chart from his pocket. "I don't think he's headed for another island. If he were, he'd run east to Makapu'u Point and then take the Molokai Express south from there. I think he's trying to rendezvous with a ship south

198

of Oahu. There's plenty of ships out there tonight. Most are trying like hell to reach Honolulu before the hurricane hits."

"Hurricane?"

"Headed north-northwest, last I heard. It's about four hundred miles south of the Big Island. It's supposed to be off Hilo by tomorrow, but it's jinxed all over the Pacific. Nobody can tell where that thing's going to end up."

"And the sailboat's last bearing was due south?"

Max smiled. It was a grim smile, more suitable to an undertaker. "Right toward it. If they keep that up they'll either run into the hurricane or they'll find their ship."

"If that happens . . ." I didn't know what else to say. If that happened, then Kate was lost, and so was any chance of retrieving the remaining tapes. Thompson would have all that remained of his tape library aboard that sailboat. Because of Kate my priorities were changing, but destroying the tapes was still high on the list.

"Wait one." I went below and retrieved my cash from the bulkhead. If I went down I didn't want this going with me. I looked at the stacks of currency, aside from *Duchess* the only wealth in the world I possessed. For the first time I was splitting my resources. I put it in a white plastic trash bag and went topside and handed it to Max. "This is yours if I don't come back."

Max didn't even look inside the bag but I could tell he knew what it was. "It'll be safe."

"Throw a party if you don't see me again. A small party. Save the rest for your retirement."

"Here." Max handed me another black box, somewhat smaller than the other and without a screen.

"What's that?"

"Another transmitter. Don't want to lose you, too."

I nodded and put the little bug in the pocket of my shorts. "Help me with the dock lines, will you?"

"Sure."

"And see if you can put in a good word with the harbor master for me."

"That's already been arranged by someone with a little more juice than I've got."

"The admiral's here?"

Max smiled. "I didn't say that," he said, unlooping the last of the dock lines. When the engine started he gave *Duchess* a shove and I was away.

"Be sure to deep-six that thing when you've found what you're looking for!" he called, meaning the direction finder. "We don't want any comebacks if it all goes wrong!"

I waved to him as *Duchess* headed toward the channel. He remained there, a lone figure on the end of the dock, until I passed the *Arizona* memorial and I couldn't see him any longer and he blended with the lines and shadows of the little marina that was my home.

$$\text{VVVVVVV}$$

33

I navigated Pearl Harbor's narrow entrance channel, squeezing to get as much clearance as possible between *Duchess* and an attack submarine on its way home. A few years back I'd spent some time as cargo aboard a nuclear submarine. It took my team from point A to point B, never mind when and never mind where. I found it too small for my liking and the view terrible. Join the navy and see the bulkhead. I saluted the colors as the two boats passed. An officer on the sail returned my salute smartly, probably annoyed by the civilian sailboat coming so close to his precious sub. It wasn't supposed to happen, but you don't see many sailboats leaving Pearl Harbor at night, either.

Once out of the channel I adjusted *Duchess*'s engine to give me the maximum speed for the stormy conditions. She was a sailboat, but tonight she would be nothing but a motor vessel. The sails would stay down. The seas were mountainous, topped with whitecaps, and we spent as much time ascending the rollers and descending into the valleys of the big swells as we did making forward speed. I found we could not make over six knots.

The ride was a tough one, but not impossible. If the hurricane moved north before this was done it would then be impossible. Right now Oahu was protected from the full force of the storm by distance and the landmass of Hawaii. Once the hurricane cleared the Big Island, the full effect of a Pacific hurricane would be felt locally. If it weren't for Kate I'd have abandoned Thompson to his fate. I didn't know what kind of a sailor he was, but his boat was so small he'd have to be a better man than I to challenge these elements. A better man, or a more desperate one.

I set my course for Barber's Point Naval Air Station. There were beacons and a coast guard station on the beach at Barber's Point. That way *Duchess* could hug the coastline and we could stay clear of the shipping lanes. And the course had the advantage of being the shortest distance between the two points.

When I got a free moment I checked the radio direction finder. The little LED screen was blank. I hoped that meant only that Thompson's boat was still on the far side of the Waianae Mountains, whose southern slopes terminated only a mile or so from Barber's Point. If I continued heading west I figured to be nearly on top of Thompson when he cleared the headlands. That was the plan anyway, tenaciously retained because it was the only one I had.

There was no moon. Thick clouds obscured the sky from horizon to horizon. The lights of Oahu on my starboard were the only illumination, stretching in an unbroken line from Honolulu all the way to Barber's Point. Far out in the shipping lanes I could see running lights of merchant vessels. They all seemed to be trying to reach safe harbor while they could. Aside from the roller coaster effect of the giant swells, it was easy. The hard part, I knew, would come later.

Duchess rolled and tossed for two hours without interruption, continuously rising and sliding through the black water, making slow, steady progress. It didn't take much skill to maintain my current course but it took a monumental effort to sit still at the wheel and wonder what was happening to Kate.

Thompson's boat was heading directly into the wind and the swells; that should keep him busy. I didn't want to think what he could be doing to her if he got bored.

In two hours *Duchess* was off the beach near the naval air station. Dawn was less than an hour away, but there was no hint of light as yet. The radio direction finder showed no reading. There was no sign of Thompson's boat. I continued west, hoping that once I cleared the headlands there would be something to guide me, and hoping Thompson hadn't sunk or met a freighter somewhere along the Waianae coast.

One of the hurricane's outer bands announced its presence with a sudden solid downpour accompanied by vicious shifting winds that shot the rain horizontally across the deck. I was instantly soaked to the skin and the rain cut the visibility to less than twenty-five yards. *Duchess*'s freeboard caught enough of the wind to heel her over toward starboard and push her bow around toward shore, where the backs of huge white breakers would break her hull as if it were eggshell. I fought the wheel, bringing her back on course.

The direction finder started beeping.

I glanced at the little screen, checked the compass mounted on the cabin's bulkhead, and then checked the screen again. If I believed the little gizmo Max provided, Thompson was dead ahead, somewhere in the gloom along my own course of travel. If he was moving, the LED would display a change in course. The rain continued, a silver curtain blown by the warm, humid winds of a tropical hurricane. The direction finder did not indicate how far off the transmitter was, that would take triangulation, but knowing which direction to go, just possessing the knowledge that the boat still existed was enough for me just then. That gave me enough to continue.

I checked the marine weather forecast. The hurricane watch had been discontinued and a hurricane warning was now in effect. All vessels, not just small craft, were advised to avoid the area and head to the nearest port. The storm was now classified category four, one of the most powerful, and in the last hour, after taking a short tour of an empty corner of the Pacific Ocean, it had begun moving toward the west coast of the island of Hawaii. The eye was still three hundred miles south of Oahu, but its effects were now being felt along the Waianae and the southern coasts of the island. Maui and its neighbors were being thrashed by rain and high winds. And the hurricane wasn't even in the neighborhood yet.

The rain stopped as abruptly as it began, leaving a hot, humid atmosphere and an oppressive ambiance behind. Dawn broke at my back, a dirty, gray light diffused with residual moisture. Warm breezes blew from my port side, providing no relief from the humidity. Visibility improved to half a mile but I could only see that far in the brief moment when *Duchess* crested a roller. The rest of the time she was sliding down the back of one wave or climbing the next, bucking and shuddering, her rigging groaning with the strain.

Once a rogue wave came in perpendicular to the wave track and I barely had time to turn her bow to quarter the monster before *Duchess* buried her nose in green water. I held on to the wheel with a death grip as she submarined through the peak of the wave and leapt free on the other side. The vortex swept away the cushions and all the other loose gear in the cockpit.

The radio direction finder went with the rest of the jetsam. Without that electronic eye, I was blind. I had no choice but to continue the same course, and assume it was correct. Just in case there were other rogues like that I tied myself to the wheel.

At the crest of a wave, out of the corner of my eye, I thought I caught something off my starboard side. Before the brain could register the event, *Duchess* was tobogganing down the back of the wave and I was bracing for the impact and the climb up the slope of the next. I looked for whatever had caught my eye the next time and saw nothing. It took three more roller coaster rides before I caught sight of a sailboat, shredded sails flying horizontally with the direction of the wind. Guides and sheets were flaying about and the mast looked cocked at an odd angle. The boat looked to be some two hundred yards away, just off my starboard quarter. I would not have seen it at all except for the coincidental cresting of both boats at the same instant. Had I not been looking in that exact direction at that exact moment it would have been missed.

I calculated an intercept and adjusted course. I wanted to come from behind. Heading into these monstrous waves would cause all of Thompson's attention to be directed forward. Given the dangers at his twelve o'clock, I hoped he wouldn't pay any attention to his six.

The sailboat was gone the next time *Duchess* crested, and also on the next two waves, but the fourth one gave me an unobstructed view of the little craft.

It was closer now, some seventy-five yards distant, and more detail was visible. As the stern disappeared over the side of its wave I saw that it was trailed by a track of cavitated water, evidence that the boat's engine was running. I also caught sight of a lone figure in the cockpit, although it was too far away to tell who it was.

The next time the boat came into view it was only twenty yards away. There was no doubt it was Thompson. In that brief glimpse his profile was unmistakable. No one else was visible. His sailboat was damaged, and it wallowed as it passed over the waves. I understood why *Duchess* had closed the gap so quickly. Thompson's boat appeared to be partially filled with water. There was little freeboard below the gunwales. It was barely making headway. Another rogue wave would sink it. Another hour of this would have the same effect.

A blast of rain swept across the ocean, blanking out visibility beyond ten yards. Thompson's boat disappeared behind a beaded curtain. *Duchess* had given me more than I could have expected, but now I asked for more. I gunned her engine and she shot forward, shuddering and popping from the strain, giving it all she had. Once, twice we rode up and over a rolling black mountain of moving water. The third time *Duchess* came crashing down behind Thompson's sailboat in a course so close her wake lifted the smaller craft and shoved it aside.

As his boat was driven from its route Thompson saw me for the first time, his face registering a satisfying mask of surprise. It must have been a shock. He'd killed me twice and yet here I was, following him to the edge of a hurricane. I was ready to follow him to the edge of hell itself. We rose over the next wave together and *Duchess* passed him. I didn't get a chance to savor the moment. Thompson and his sailboat disappeared in our wake.

I cut the engine back to minimal revolutions but inertia continued driving *Duchess* ahead. My attempt at slowing her caused green water to break over the bow. Without sufficient forward momentum, *Duchess* became a toy of the ocean. Too much of this and she would be as waterlogged as Thompson's boat, but if I increased speed I'd never get back to him, or to Kate. They couldn't last much longer. But neither could *Duchess*.

I didn't want to think about the return voyage with huge and erratic following seas. As far as I could tell we'd already reached the point of no return. In the last report I'd heard, the hurricane was moving north at better than thirty knots. In these seas *Duchess* could not make better than six. That presented a simple logistical problem that would not go away. But it wouldn't be a problem unless I could get Kate off Thompson's boat. I'd consider my mission accomplished if I could just leave him and his boat and all it contained out here. The storm would swallow him forever.

The next roller brought us nearly to a stop in the bottom of the trough. A wave crested above us, nearly as high as *Duchess*'s mast. She started to slip sideways, a move that would capsize her. I gunned the engine, hoping to bring her bow into the wave. When it broke she was forty-five degrees to the wave's direction of travel and she capsized. White foaming pressure hit like a wall of concrete falling from the sky, then there was a bottle green light, a painful pressure on the ears and a sense of disorientation, and then the battleship gray skies overhead once again as *Duchess*'s heavy keel did what it was designed to do. Gravity did not exist in those moments, replaced by a curious fatalism. *Duchess* would rise or she would not. Whatever happened, we would ride it out together.

When she righted herself I did a quick inventory of the damage. Her masts and rigging had vanished, swept away as neatly as if they'd been transported by a magician. All the rest of my topside gear was gone. Her engine had quit. But we were floating.

I tried starting the engine but it was dead. I grabbed the two-man inflatable life support raft from the cockpit storage locker. It was an improvement on the older life rafts because it had a complete watertight enclosure. It wouldn't swamp. It also had an automatic strobe light and transmitter with new batteries good for twenty hours of constant use. I didn't know if it would survive this kind of sea but there wasn't an alternative. It was all I had. I slipped the safety loop over my left shoulder.

Duchess slid down the retreating side of another wave. Despite the damage she'd suffered, she met the next one head on, bursting through the crown like the thoroughbred she was. I looked back for Thompson's boat and found to my horror that he was coming on, less than five yards from my stern, about to crash into *Duchess*.

I braced for the collision. The bow of Thompson's boat smashed through the railing of *Duchess*'s stern, burying itself into the wooden hull structure below the cockpit. Reacting, not thinking, I jumped for his bowsprit, rolled to the top and hung on. The two boats were like mating behemoths, hinged at the larger one's stern, the vicious wave action working them back and forth. I climbed aboard the smaller craft just before she slipped off my boat. *Duchess* was on her own. I never looked back, afraid of what I might see.

VVVVVVV

34

Thompson was too busy to notice me scramble aboard. For a moment I nearly lost my grip when the next comber crashed down upon us, sending both boats spinning in the trough. Green frothy water sent me slithering along the slick fiberglass roof of the cabin, nearly washing me overboard until I found a handhold.

When the water cleared I discovered I'd been grasping an edge of the forward hatch. I opened it and jackknifed inside, hauling the inflatable package with me. I landed on the forward bunk. Before the next wave rolled across the deck I shut the hatch and dogged it down tight.

I was aware of a small body lying next to me. Kate lay on her side, tossed in the corner like a discarded rag doll. Her eyes were closed and she was so still and quiet I thought she was dead. I put my ear next to her mouth and listened to shallow, rapid breathing. Her pulse was quick and weak. Her face was the color of oatmeal. When I checked her I found a wet, spongy spot in her skull behind her left ear.

"Kate!"

She didn't move. Whatever was going on in the irreplaceable gray jelly of her brain wasn't registering my voice, or was incapable of answering.

"Kate!"

There was no response. I had seen concussion before. Unless she could get medical attention soon there would never be any response again.

I watched for Thompson and the other man who had been described boarding this boat. Looking through the aft porthole I could see part of Thompson's leg as he struggled with the wheel. Of the other man I could see nothing. He had either been swept overboard by accident or Thompson had eliminated him, further lowering his overhead. It didn't matter. Either way it was only the two of us now. And the sea would play the winner.

I searched the tiny cabin. I'd taken no weapons with me when I jumped other than the little .357 magnum derringer and my Buck Folding Hunter. The derringer had all four barrels loaded. Everything else I owned was aboard *Duchess*. It began to look like everything I owned would soon be at the bottom of the Pacific.

Water-soaked cardboard boxes were piled on the floor and the settee in the lounge, piled all the way to the overhead. They would be Thompson's master tape library. Other boxes lined the deck. They were more sturdy, made of wood and banded by double metal straps. I tried to lift one and found it almost too heavy for one man. Few common metals have that weight: lead, uranium or gold. I guessed gold. Seven boxes of the stuff were going to the bottom with us, more bounty to be found by some future treasure hunter with an ability to get to eight thousand feet.

Sitting on top of the boxes of gold was a crocodile leather briefcase. It was locked, but it was relatively easy to open with a church key I found in one of the galley drawers. Inside the sodden leather case were many small manila envelopes. Each envelope had an abbreviated script scrawled across it. One said, 2 CT. VVS1. I opened it and found a diamond whose brilliance reflected fire even in the darkened cabin.

There were over a hundred of the little packets. I had no idea what the value of a diamond was, but I knew that one this size, if it was perfect, could be worth more than five thousand dollars a carat. I estimated the value of the briefcase to be close to a million dollars. This was the bulk of Thompson's movable retirement fund. It was perfect for him: small, portable, unreportable and untraceable; better than cash. On impulse I decided to take it along. If it was good for Thompson, it would be even better for me.

Taking the briefcase, I crawled to the forward berth and lifted Kate from her bunk, carefully cradling her head. Her respiration was so quiet I had to put my ear to her mouth again to make certain she still survived. I opened the overhead hatch and maneuvered her onto the deck, keeping low and trying to keep from washing overboard at the same time. Thompson hadn't seen me yet. When he did he would react. I didn't need the complication. Getting off this boat with Kate was my only priority. If I didn't have to deal with Thompson, so much the better. This boat wouldn't last and I'd be happy to let the elements finish the job.

When I had Kate tied off I reached below and grabbed the briefcase. Another wave poured over the bow, pushing us underwater so long I thought the boat had been sucked down for good. The boat's positive buoyancy finally overcame the weight of the sea and rose to the surface again, giving me a chance for a single breath before the next one buried us.

The boat remained under longer with each successive wave. I'd left the hatch open and water was filling the air space below. A few more waves and it would be gone. The next time we were underwater I untied Kate and the briefcase and pulled the D-ring on the life raft. It inflated immediately, but too late to rise above the hull. A fluke caused that wave to be shallow, and the life raft inflated on deck, twisting and trapping the little doughnut of air in the stainless steel deck lines. As I worked to untangle the steel cables from the raft I heard a hoarse cry. Thompson had seen us.

A bullet struck the deck inches from my leg, nearly taking off my knee. Two more little wasps buzzed by my ear. Galvanized by adrenaline, I placed Kate into the habitable space of the raft, tossed the briefcase in after her, and shoved the raft into the sea. Another shot plunked into the water near the raft before the crest of the next wave washed over us, knocking me off my feet. The raft bobbed away in the turbulence, the wind rapidly pushing it toward Oahu. I grabbed for a handhold but was washed toward the cockpit.

The force of the wave ripped me along the length of the boat, bouncing me between steel stanchions and the cabin wall. I crashed against something solid and was pinned against it by the weight of the water. When it subsided I found myself upside down beneath Thompson's feet.

He would have killed me, but he was entangled in the safety railing. He knew I was there but couldn't get at me. I reached for the derringer in the hip pocket of my shorts but it was gone.

Thompson kicked me in the chin. Stars exploded in my head. His second kick struck my right shoulder. Something collapsed inside, lighting up a fiery agony. My vision dimmed around the edges.

Another wave flooded the cockpit and knocked him back against the railing. I was aware that the boat was settling deeper. Water didn't drain from the scuppers anymore. Now it flowed in from the sea.

Because I was protected by the cabin superstructure I was the first to regain my balance. Thompson saw me on my feet and with a superhuman effort fought against the wave and righted himself. He still held an automatic pistol. He aimed it at my face and pulled the trigger. Nothing happened.

"You! You fuck! You fucked me!" Fury swelled him, making the muscles along his jaw rigid with the emotion. I could almost smell his anger. He pulled the trigger again, and again nothing happened. He threw the pistol at me. It bounced off my chest.

He had something else to say but I didn't want to hear it. In a single, practiced motion my hand went into the right front pocket of my shorts and brought out the Buck knife. A flick of the wrist locked the blade in place as my hand was rising toward him. Before Thompson could react I stabbed him in the solar plexus, just under the rib cage, up through the heart, pushing the blade all the way to the brass pommel. He was dead before I withdrew the knife and the next wave washed him away and he was gone, vanished as if he'd never been.

As I stood there watching for sign of Thompson, the biggest wave yet rose before the bow of the little sloop. It was twice the height of the aluminum mast. When the boat rolled nearly vertical I made an instant decision. I reached into a cockpit locker, grabbed two life vests and dove into the water. I got four strokes away before the wave broke and the world was transformed into white, pounding turbulence.

I tumbled inside the maelstrom until it subsided and I could surface. Unlike Thompson's boat I'd been near the top of the swell when it broke and my natural buoyancy had been aided by the vests. The boat's positive buoyancy had been almost zero when the wave broke over it, and it remained toward the bottom of the trough.

This time it didn't come back and I was alone in the middle of the mountains of the sea.

A Sea King helicopter picked me up about noon. Max found me by triangulating the little transmitting beacon he'd given me the night before. Conditions were calmer. The hurricane had shifted again and was heading west, toward Wake Island. Local conditions had been downgraded to tropical storm intensities.

Aboard the helicopter I learned that Kate had been picked up earlier by the coast guard and had been rushed to Queens

Medical Center for an emergency operation to relieve the mounting pressure of a massive traumatic cerebral hemorrhage. I refused to cooperate with anyone until I knew her condition and then I became an immense pain in the ass until they took me to Queens. Max ran interference with law enforcement while I waited.

We were still there five hours later when the big policeman who frisked me at Kelly's that first day I met Kate came into the room and told me to come with him. Max blocked access and I thought there would be a fight until the policeman, whose name I learned was Kimo Kahanamoku, relented.

"She's not comin' back, Mr. Caine," he said. "Doctor told me a few minutes ago. They did all they could do. They couldn't do nothin'."

It was like being hit in the chest with a fist. Max put his arms around me and pulled me tightly into an embrace. "It's over, John," he said.

The room lights dimmed, gone blurry by water that suddenly filled my eyes. I nodded absently, thinking of the little time we'd spent together. There wouldn't be a chance to see her again, to feel her touch, hold her hand, smell her hair or feel her breath on my neck and her body against mine. All the solid, powerful essence of her was gone. There wouldn't even be a chance to say goodbye. She was gone. We have so little time here and there's such a long, long time afterward. Like forever. I wanted us to have more. I wasn't ready to lose her.

And I was suddenly ashamed of myself. It wasn't just my loss. It was also hers. Kate didn't want to die. It was not her intention to slide off into that uncertain blackness alone. She'd wanted to live, too.

"Yeah," I said. "I guess it's over."

"You gonna come with me now?"

"I don't think so," said Max. "He's already in federal custody. Mr. Caine won't be going anywhere."

Kahanamoku nodded. "We thought you'd say that," he said. "There's a federal judge who's issued a warrant. That means he's coming with me."

Max looked at his watch. "How old is that warrant?"

The big policeman shook his head. "I dunno. Couple hours. Why?"

"Check with the judge. See if it's been canceled."

There was a brief staring contest. Neither man was accustomed to bluffing. Each man saw that in the other. Kahanamoku nodded. "I'll check. You two wait here."

Max put his arm around my shoulders. "We'll be here, Lieutenant, when you get back. You can bet on it."

$$\vee\vee\vee\vee\vee\vee\vee$$

35

They say that no good deed goes unpunished. A corollary to that should be: The greater the good, the harsher the punishment. I'd gambled almost everything and lost everything I'd gambled, but in the end I'd succeeded, to a point, and that point meant everything. Admiral MacGruder's reputation and that of his daughter remained intact and her killer had been quietly punished. Evidence of Mary MacGruder's disintegration had either burned or gone to the bottom of the Pacific.

Thompson spoke of winners and losers. He'd lost, I'd won, although the difference between the two of us was mere survival. That being the case, then Kate had lost, too, and I'd lost Kate. The Pyrrhic cost of my success was something I was not yet ready to contemplate too closely. I'd lost the one thing that meant anything to me in this whole event. Maybe, in the end, survival was the only thing that really mattered.

Numb from the sheer magnitude of the loss, I plodded through the next few days, facing whatever happened. The experience was not all that new to me. I'd been here before. If survival were to be my only reward, then surviving each day seemed wholly appropriate. To mark the time I started a beard, a measure of my days of confinement.

There were many questions to be answered, many questions

from many people from many different agencies, because there was, as one investigator put it, a basic question of jurisdiction. Kimo Kahanamoku, the Honolulu police detective, took a special interest in my interrogation and after a silent, internecine struggle between the relevant law enforcement agencies I understood he finally had the lead in the combined investigations.

Someone arranged temporary accommodation for me in transient officer's quarters at Makalapa. It didn't shelter me from law enforcement but it did keep the media types away. I wasn't officially under arrest, but it was clear that I wasn't supposed to leave the CINCPAC compound, either. That wasn't a problem. I had nowhere to go and no way to get there. I was provided unmarked utilities to wear. From my window I could see a portion of the little marina that had been my home for over a decade. It might as well have been a photograph of a Martian landscape. I couldn't go there, and had I been able to leave the base there was nothing to go to. I spent my days speaking to detectives and federal investigators, and I passed my nights staring at the ceiling and thinking of Kate, thinking about what would have happened if . . .

If is a terrible word.

A week after Kate died, Kimo came to my quarters. He brought me civilian clothes, pants and shoes and a loud Hawaiian shirt and tersely told me to put them on. I dressed while he watched, followed him to his car, and allowed him to drive me to the InterIsland Terminal at Honolulu Airport. We flew in a tiny Aloha Airlines prop plane to Princeville on the north shore of Kauai. He said little. During most of the flight he stared mutely out the porthole at the ocean below.

It was one of those breathtaking, spectacular Hawaiian days of sunshine and warm breezes, the kind of day pictured in hotel brochures and sugar cane commercials. We were met at the airport by a large Hawaiian man wearing ratty shorts and a clean white dress shirt. He was barefoot and heavily bearded, and what was visible of his face, arms and legs was decorated with crude tattoos. His graying black hair hung nearly to his waist. He gave us open-ended leis made from aromatic maile leaves, draping them around our necks in a solemn ceremony. He gave Kimo a bear hug and gently shook my hand, as if he were aware of my injuries. He knew my name and introduced himself simply as Ed. Ed had an ancient green pickup parked in the lot. I crawled in between the two giants and we headed west on the two-lane highway toward Hanalei.

"Your name is Caine," Ed said. He had a deep rumbling voice that matched his bulk, a voice that carried a kind of natural authority. Ed was used to talking and having other people listen. I guessed his age at around fifty, but he had seen a lot of sun and a lot of living and he looked at least a decade older. "You know the Bible?"

I nodded, understanding the reference.

"Cain was a farmer. He tilled the soil until his brother tried to take it away from him. Do you know this passage?"

"I've read it."

"Ah, a reader. Then you know that Cain killed his brother, Abel. He was cursed by God to wander the earth forever. He was the man who was closest to the earth, and his punishment was never to have a home of his own. Is that you, Caine? Did you kill your brother? Is that why you're cursed?"

"I never had a brother."

"All men are brothers."

I'd heard people talk about my name before, as if it had some significance. I was descended from Welsh-English stock who came to America in the late nineteenth century. The name had existed for as long as anyone in the family could remember. I was the last of the line. My parents were dead and I'd had no children. I glanced at Kimo. He was looking out the window.

"*Kane*," Ed said. He pronounced it Kah-nay, accenting the first syllable. "That's the Hawaiian language. Do you know what *kane* means?"

"It means 'man,' " I said.

"You're right. Kane was the basic man. Kind of like a Hawaiian Adam. Not all Caines are bad, you know. You are not an evil man. I can see that. You may have done bad things, but you're not a bad man."

"Thank you."

"Kimo tells me you saved Kate Alapai. Is that right?"

"I tried. If I were faster or smarter I would have succeeded."

"You sailed into a hurricane and took her away from an evil man."

"I didn't save her life."

"You did everything you could. Kimo and I thought you should attend my sister's memorial service."

I looked at Kimo again. He did not look in my direction.

"Your sister."

"Kimo is my best friend. He is also my cousin. His mother's sister was my uncle's sister on my mother's side. We are not really related, but we're close. My family name is Alapai. Do you know the significance of that?"

"No."

"It is from Alapa. The Alapa Guard were King Kamehameha's personal bodyguard. They were chosen from the largest and the most fierce warriors he could find. We three are direct descendants, some of the only ones left. What Kate lacked in big, she made up in fierce. She was a warrior, as you are a warrior. You would have been well matched."

"She told you about me."

Alapai nodded. "As did Kimo. He looked after Kate. We are a close family, and she spoke about the two of you. She thought you might have had a future, even though you disappointed her when you took off on your own. But even that she understood."

Kimo shook his head. "I had less than five minutes to speak with her when *Pele* came up empty. She knew you had another agenda, and she told me she would have been disappointed if you'd done anything else." I noticed that once he approved of me, Kimo's pidgin disappeared.

Ed Alapai said, "Kimo says you have friends in high places. He received a visit from a very interesting gentleman. An admiral in the United States Navy."

"He was accompanied by a very senior noncommissioned officer," said Kimo. "A man you know."

"Max."

"Yes. Senior Chief Maximilian White. They both told me some things that helped your case."

"My case."

Kimo nodded. "The coast guard wanted to charge you with piracy. That's still a capital offense. Then the alphabet soup agencies wanted to charge you with a variety of crimes that would have landed your ass in a federal penitentiary for the rest of your natural life. I wanted to hang you for murder, but I found myself at the back of the line. For a while.

"Your friends let me know some of the facts. I didn't know everything Kate was working on. I was her supervisor and I didn't know how deeply she was into this case, or the extent of the damage. She and Captain Yoshida knew things that they didn't share. When they died, well, it just wasn't there anymore.

"You helped put down one real bad man. We solved over thirty murders and missing persons. All little girls. The admiral told me some of the details. In the end it was decided that you saved the taxpayers the cost of a trial. It helped that the admiral spoke for you, though."

"Is that an understatement?"

The big policeman nodded. "Yeah. That's an understatement. But what helped you the most was the United States Attorney said you'd most likely walk if you went to trial. Did you know that Thompson tried to blackmail MacGruder?"

"He bragged about it."

"That's when your friend, the chief, got involved. He went to you and asked your help." Kimo was silent for a moment. "You go back a long way." It was a declaration. When I was silent he continued. "Back to Vietnam?"

"Yes."

"Always a SEAL?"

"Yes."

"You're a real hard case, aren't you?"

"Not anymore," I said.

"Yeah, well, maybe you get over it."

"I liked Kate."

"Liked? She was in love with you, man. That's why you're here. You were someone she could trust. Do you know how rare that was for her?"

"And I couldn't save her."

"Don't beat yourself up, Caine," said Alapai. "She knew the risks. You brought her back. She would have been lost from us forever."

The truck bounced off the paved road onto a red dirt track across a field of grass. A small group of people were gathered in the field near the edge of a cliff. Beyond was the Pacific, its calm blue surface showing no trace of the storm. A warm, gentle breeze blew in from the sea, carrying the scent of salt and kiawe and the tangy smell of passion fruit.

The truck stopped near the other cars, a collection of ancient local transportation. We got out and walked toward the assembly of men and women and children. They looked like an extended family, and I realized that was exactly what they were. They were dressed in casual clothes, old shorts like Ed Alapai's or lightweight trousers. Tees and short-sleeved shirts predominated. Mine was the only Hawaiian shirt, I wore the only shoes and I was the only haole, the only outsider.

The service was brief. Ed Alapai said a few words, and

chanted an ancient chant that seemed to come directly from the days of King Kamehameha. He sang it first in English and then in Hawaiian. I remembered a few details about a tiger shark, resting without fear and a girl with flashing eyes and a restless, questing gaze. The girl was Mary MacGruder. She was Kate. She was all the little girls who'd been abused and then murdered. I didn't retain any more of the chant. Tears stung my eyes. There was no tune, but Alapai's passion made me feel his loss, and mine. For a short time we were all brothers and I was a part of the family.

Kimo had brought Kate's ashes in a small box and when the breeze changed, sprinkled them from the top of the cliff where they scattered over the ocean. In a few moments the mortal remains of the woman who had briefly loved me were merged with the earth.

When all the others were gone Kimo Kahanamoku, Ed Alapai and I stood on the edge of the cliff. Bright clouds scudded across the horizon in neat formations with dark, flat bottoms and white, billowy tops. A lone albatross fluttered in from the open ocean, saw us standing near its nest and fled.

"Kate had something with her when the coast guard picked her up. Do you know anything about that?" Kimo watched the albatross attempt another landing. She seemed desperate to get to her nest, but she was not brave enough to challenge us. He smiled and walked away from the edge of the cliff.

"A briefcase."

When we were a distance from her nest, the albatross landed and scurried across the tall grass toward her chicks.

"It wasn't Kate's. Was it yours?"

"I guess so."

"You guess so. Can you describe it?"

"Brown leather. Alligator."

Kimo nodded. "Not crocodile?"

"That's illegal."

He smiled. "Alligator. Okay. You're sure it's yours."

"Yes."

"You left another briefcase at her apartment. That's yours, too?"

I nodded.

"Yeah, it had your wallet in it. When we get back you can have them. Both of them."

"Just like that?"

"Just like that. Call it whatever you want. When we get back you're free to go."

"No charges?"

"None. You did us some favors. Why bring up stuff that should remain buried?"

"You may come back." Ed Alapai put his hand on my shoulder. "I live on Anahola Mountain. There is a *heiau* up there that needs attention. You can weed taro. Let your soul heal. It's been wounded, same as you." He pointed to my broken shoulder and the burns on my face and hands. "I know you will not stay forever, but you must rest awhile before you go on. A warrior must rest sometime."

"I will come back," I said. "After I take care of some business in Honolulu."

He nodded. "The land is sacred and can heal. Even though a Cain is cursed and must wander the earth, you're welcome on this land. You're family now, a kane. You're not cursed on this island. Give your *mana* to the land, and the land will make you strong again." He embraced me. "I will be waiting."

VVVVVVV

36

I parked my Jeep in the five-dollar lot near the taxi stand off Beretania. Taking my briefcase, I walked to the restaurant on River Street. It was late afternoon and the restaurant was nearly deserted. I took possession of a corner booth, ordered tea and waited. Chawlie wasn't in, but I expected he'd show up soon enough.

Twenty minutes later the old man came in from his back room, blinking in the light like a displaced owl. He saw me at once and shuffled to my booth.

"You really are a barbarian now, John Caine," Chawlie said, fingering his own chin whiskers.

"I got lazy in captivity."

"You live dangerously," he said, sliding into the seat across from me.

"No longer, Uncle," I said. "I have a business proposition for you."

Chawlie's eyes narrowed. "No do business with you anymore. You die tomorrow, tonight, mebbe next week, I don't know. You let people shoot you again, sink your boat, burn you up. What next? You very bad risk. You are very unstable man. Not good for business partner."

"I'm alive. Thompson is not."

"You kill him?"

"Yes."

He considered it. "Still. No deal. You find someone not as old as you, he can take you easy."

"I know some that probably could," I said. "This is different." I opened my briefcase and removed a handful of the little manila envelopes. His eyes widened when I shook their contents onto the table. The glistening stones lay in a pile, quickly swept together, hidden by deft hands while his eyes searched the room for witnesses to my foolish act.

"These real?"

"Yes."

"Most of these two carats!"

"If you say so," I said. "I'm no expert on diamonds."

He picked one and held it to the light. A kaleidoscope of color burst from the stone. In spite of himself, Chawlie smiled.

"Where you get this?"

"Thompson. I stole them."

His smile widened. "You steal these before you kill him or after?"

"Before."

"He know you did it?"

"Yes."

"You good man, John Caine! You be my partner!"

"How much are these worth?"

He moved the diamonds around the tabletop, arranging them in patterns, losing himself in the game. I'd counted one hundred forty-eight stones, all approximately two carats. Some were bigger. I'd made a quick stop at a jeweler at Ala Moana and asked what a two-carat VVS1 stone was worth, reading what was written on the envelope. I figured wholesale at around four thousand dollars a carat. That would make each stone worth from sixty-five hundred to ten thousand dollars.

"Oh, diamond market not very good these days," said Chawlie at last. "Can probably get five hundred a carat."

I started picking up the stones from the scarred tabletop. One became lodged in a deep gouge in the wood and lay there reflecting the afternoon sun. I saw why people became enamored of diamonds. It held a beautiful cold fire, like a portable rainbow you could call up at will.

"No! I find out! I mebbe wrong, John Caine!"

"Yeah. You're maybe wrong. Try again."

"Two thousand! Tops, mebbe three."

I continued picking up the diamonds, one at a time, lingering when my fingers brushed the slanting beam of sunlight that came through the front window.

"I give you five thousand each stone! I take all risk on selling."

I thought about it. Five thousand dollars a stone. Close to three quarters of a million dollars. About half what they were worth. Chawlie was offering to split the take with me fifty-fifty. It wasn't as much as I could have received if I sold them one at a time, but it was better than expected and nearly what I needed.

"I'm no merchant," I said. "Cash. Three days."

"I can do, John Caine. You give me now, I pay you three days time."

"Of course, Chawlie. You good risk. Nobody ever shoot you, eh?"

He smiled, a wide, toothy grin. "Thompson make you rich, yah? He always talk winners and losers, winners and losers. He big loser."

I nodded.

"As big as it gets," I said.

VVVVVVVV

37

There was an unoccupied table in the corner of the Marina, the open-air restaurant at the top of the slip where *Duchess* used to dock. The sun had vanished behind the Waianae Mountains by the time I got there, and there were no breezes in the warm summer night. The Kona winds had come again, bringing a close, sticky humidity without the cleansing trade winds that usually grace these islands. The night was black. Only the orange sodium lights of Makakilo and Pearl City lined the great darkness that was Pearl Harbor.

Max had called me on my cellular telephone as I was leaving Chawlie's place. He was on the island, he had my money, and the admiral wanted to talk to me. I agreed to meet them at the Marina. I didn't know why, but when I thought about it I guessed it was because it felt comfortable there. It had, after all, been a part of my life for more than a decade.

Max and Admiral MacGruder arrived ten minutes after I did. Max was in full dress uniform, wearing all his ribbons, and carrying a briefcase. He was impressive. I recognized the admiral immediately, even though he'd lost considerable weight since I'd last seen him. He had graying, close-cropped hair on a narrow skull. His build was spare and skinny, like a marathon runner or a terminal cancer patient. He saw me and smiled. It was a sad kind of smile. This man did not naturally view the world as a happy place. When I stood at his approach, I noticed he no longer had the ramrod posture I'd remembered.

"Mr. Caine."

"Call me John, Admiral."

"Call me Winston, John. You're no longer in uniform."

"Yes, sir," I said.

It was a little joke, meant to relax him. It was also intended to let him know the depth of respect and affection I had for him. A waitress came and the admiral ordered a bottle of Opus One cabernet sauvignon. Max shook his head and ordered a Corona Extra.

"Max told me your story. At least part of it. I can't tell you how much I appreciate . . . what you did. There are no words, John. No words."

"I owed you, sir."

Our drinks arrived, and we sat in silence while the bottles were opened. When the waitress left he said, "Most people wouldn't understand that."

"Some debts cannot be discharged any other way," I said.

"That's true, as far as it goes. But now I am in your debt."

I shook my head. "Not at all."

"You suffered great loss."

"You have, too."

"It is impossible," he said, "getting through life without some loss. The chief here has something that belongs to you."

Max reached under the table and handed me the black leather briefcase. "It's all there, John," said Max. "Plus a little."

"There's no way for me to adequately reward you, John. The money you gave to Max for safekeeping is there, as is a check to compensate you for the loss of your home." When I began to protest, he put up his hand to stop me. "It's only right," he said. "I've enough money. It's the right thing to do."

So what do you say to that? I said thank you and took another sip of the cabernet.

"You suffered another loss, I'm told. Kate Alapai, the detective, wasn't it? I met her. She was a fine woman. I'm sorry for your loss. I know what it's like."

"It all hasn't hit me yet, Admiral. I'm just taking it one day at a time."

"Yes," he said. "That's the only way to do it. Have you had a chance to make any plans?"

I shook my head. "I'm going to Kauai in a couple of days. I'll spend as much time as it takes. There's a heiau there, and some of Kate's people are restoring it. They invited me to work with them. Work on the stones, weed the taro patch. You know, carry water, chop wood. Right now it sounds good."

"Weed taro? Like Scipio Africanus, the general-farmer who saved Rome from Hannibal? I can see you doing that for a short time. Then you'll have to do something else."

"It will do for now. I need to find some peace."

The admiral nodded, his lips pursed into a thin line. He too needed peace. I hoped that I'd given him a chance, now that there were no longer uncertainties about his daughter. "Max tells me you do this kind of thing for a living," he said. "When you feel up to it, give me a call. I might have something for you."

"I might retire."

"You may, but I doubt it." MacGruder stood up. "I've taken enough of your time, John. Finish the bottle. Max and I have to get back to Coronado. There are some things that need our attention, or at least that's what people believe. We don't wish for them to find out otherwise, now do we?"

"Thompson tried to blackmail you, didn't he?"

There was a pause, and then he said, "Yes. He sent me a copy of a tape with Mary in it. It was, ah, not a pleasant experience. He followed up with a phone call, demanding money, threatening to ruin me."

"Is that when you sent Max to see me?"

His gray eyes became steely. "Max did that on his own,

John. I would never have considered asking you to do what you did. I could never do that. Max didn't tell me about your involvement until you had left Pearl Harbor and were out chasing Thompson. By then all I could do was smooth the waters for you a little and get the law enforcement types off your back when you returned."

"Thank you for that."

"I didn't send Max. He came on his own. Sometimes he listens to my telephone conversations. He heard Thompson's threat. And I found that out only after the fact. Max knew Mary and it hurt him to see what had happened to her, and what Thompson was trying to do to me."

Max had been quiet up to this point, and he leaned forward on massive forearms. "John, the man's telling the truth. He didn't know I was here. That's why I only had one day to find you. And here you are. Guess I had the right idea. You know if Thompson had been arrested, and he got one of those asshole lawyers they have these days, he'd put Mary on trial. Thompson would have dragged everybody down with him, and the admiral would have gone down, too. This way it's over, and it stays over."

I nodded. Except Kate wasn't with me, and never would be again. "I understand," I said. "You did the best you could. Goodbye, Admiral. I hope to see you someday. Under better circumstances."

He shook my hand. I was happy to see he still had a firm grip. Maybe he would get better. That's what this was supposed to be all about, anyway. "Call me if you get bored, John, or if you need anything."

As he left, Max patted me on the shoulder. "Well, sailor boy, you did good. I'm sorry about Kate. These things don't always work out for everybody."

"She was doing her job, Max. That's all I can say right now."

"You can reach the admiral through me. I'll be there if you ever need anything. And so will he. He owes you now, John.

And so do I." He followed MacGruder, leaving me with my thoughts and the bottle of wine. And the briefcase. I opened it and saw neat banded stacks of currency. It looked like the same money I'd given Max. There was an envelope, too; a slim, cream-colored no. ten, and it was unsealed.

I picked it up and lifted the flap. Inside was a light blue certified check from something called WMG Holding Company payable to me in the amount of two hundred fifty thousand dollars. It was more than *Duchess* was worth, including the contents. I closed the briefcase and locked it. There would be time to consider it. There would be time to consider all of it. But not now. Not tonight. Maybe not for a long time. I reached for the bottle and filled my glass.

$$\vee\vee\vee\vee\vee\vee\vee\vee$$

FOUR MONTHS LATER

T he wall looks good." Ed Alapai delivered a slap on the back
with his judgment. I was proud of my reconstruction of
the ancient wall of the heiau and it gratified me that he approved. "This is good, Kane, you know?" Alapai always referred
to me as Kane. Not since Kate's memorial service did he call
me by my name. It was his way of showing approval, his way
of taking me into the family.

I was sweating under a December sun. This far north the
Hawaiian sun could still be brutal even in winter.

"Here, man, it looks like you need it." He handed me a
water bottle. "Come into the trees. Only a commoner works in
the sun like that."

"Well, call me a commoner," I said.

"You're leaving," said Alapai when we'd settled in the shade
of a banyan tree. It wasn't native, but we'd decided to leave it
as it shaded the heiau all year round. It even provided protection from rainstorms. Mosquitoes left us alone. That was one
of the mysteries of this place. Mosquitoes always attacked in the
shade. But they didn't here.

"You knew."

He nodded. "I could see the signs, man. We're not done
here, but we've made progress. You've helped." The temple

site, on the northern flank of Anahola Mountain, had been covered by jungle growth and shrubs when Ed found it. He had already cleared an impressive area alone, with just his machete, before I arrived. Together we had uncovered more ancient structures, one of which I'd taken on as my project, and I reconstructed its black lava rock walls. It was hard work, demanding of both mind and body, just what I needed. As my injuries healed and my spirit mended it became easier.

"How long have you known?"

"When did you first think about leaving?"

"The thought hit me last week, when we went into town for groceries."

"You were looking at the newspapers. I knew then."

I nodded. He was right. That was when the idea solidified. It had been building over the past month, gaining strength, but I didn't recognize it for what it was. When I saw the headlines of the happenings away from this island paradise and felt a hunger for information, I knew that my isolation was no longer necessary.

"When will you leave?"

"Can you take me to the airport tomorrow morning?"

"Yes," he said. He raised his arms to enfold the forest around us, encompassing the north shore of Kauai. "It will be here for you when you need to come back." He smiled, a fierce, grim smile of a warrior-priest from outside of time. "And you will find the need to return. I know you, brother. You will come to miss Kauai as you do Kate. There will be always a longing for this place. And here you will always be welcome." The big man got to his feet. "Wait here a moment. Relax in the shade while I get something."

I slumped against the log and rested while he walked down to the little house where he lived with his family. The house was the first thing we built. Before I came they had been living in a rough A-frame that was little more than a tent. With some of the money recovered from the diamonds we built a sturdy two-room pole house with indoor plumbing and a solar water heater. I split the rest of the diamond recovery with him fifty-fifty. That would have been Kate's share and since Ed Alapai was her closest living relative it was all I could do. As the admiral had said, it was only right.

I was nearly asleep when he returned. "I have a gift for you." Ed handed me a small wooden object. It was smooth to the touch, and had a hole drilled through the small end for a string woven from rough fibers. "This is a *paloa*. That means 'tongue.' It represents friendship and trust."

I took the paloa and hung it around my neck.

"You will be Cain, again," said the big man. "Condemned to roam the earth. That seems to be your curse. But always remember you now have a place to come home to."

I nodded. I tried to say something, but my throat closed upon itself.

"It's to go with you on your travels and to remind you of us, of home. Someday, my friend, you will find what you are searching for."

"And what's that?"

"Peace. And a good woman. You can't have one without the other, you know."

"They keep killing them off."

He nodded. "That's why the good ones are so rare."

"Tomorrow morning."

"There's a flight out of Lihue to Honolulu at seven-thirty. That early enough?"

"Sure."

"Where are you going?"

"San Diego, I think. That's where I was headed when I came to Hawaii with *Duchess*. I think I'll buy a new boat. Maybe drop in on Max."

"Kimo tells me he's a good man."

"One of the best."

"So you're a rich man, *Kane*. You got good friends, and you had love. You got money. What more could you want?"

"She's out there," I said, pointing toward the ocean beyond the green cliff face of Anahola Mountain. "Use your magic. Bring her back."

"I wish I could. I miss her, too." He shook his head. "Better get back to work. Clean your tools and we'll run down to the beach to clean off this sweat. Last time for you. On the way back we'll buy beer, chips, maybe a ham. Have some friends over tonight. Throw a party, a luau. Do a little dancing. Give you a send-off in style. That sound good to you?"

It did.